A MAN'S HONOR

When news of Fort Sumter reached Two Trees, Coy Quillen was one of the first to sign up. Not many people understood his decision to join the Union forces, but Coy Quillen was a man who lived by his beliefs, and he was respected for it.

After the long, bloody years of fighting were over, Quillen came back home, a useless saber-scarred hand at his side. But this was not his worst burden. His father was dead, their ranch lost; his own brother wouldn't speak to him; his girl "belonged" to the dance hall owner.

He couldn't ally himself with the Federal troops who ruled and exploited the town; the townspeople would now have nothing to do with a man who had "fought against his own."

Coy Quillen should have left Two Trees for good, but that would be admitting the worst kind of defeat—when a man can no longer believe in himself.

Also by E.M. Parsons

The Easy Gun
Fargo
Dark of Summer

As Philip Race

Self-Made Widow
Killer Take All
Johnny Come Deadly

TEXAS HELLER

E.M. PARSONS

CUTTING EDGE

ISBN-13: 978-1-952138-45-4

Published by
Cutting Edge Publishing
PO Box 8212
Calabasas, CA 91372
www.cuttingedgebooks.com

To RUSSELL ROUSE
for his talented tolerance

CHAPTER 1

THE HORSE was dead. A dark stream furrowed the coarse neck hair and dripped to the dust of the road. Quillen fumbled the pistol into his holster with his left hand. Clumsy. Almost four years and still he hadn't found the knack.

A low rumble of hoofbeats brought him up. He searched the plain, finally found the single rider with his eyes. About a mile away. Coming at an easy lope. Quillen squinted in the flat-land glare and turned, estimating the distance remaining to the town. Not far.

Two Trees had grown. To Coy Quillen, standing on the gentle rise of plateau which swept eastward from the town, it seemed much larger than he remembered. He shaded his eyes against the afternoon sun and surveyed the tiny crossroads.

Two Trees nestled in a rolling curve of the panhandle plain as in a cupped palm. Yet it was not a valley that held the town; but a sere wrinkle in the unrelenting face of the Edward's plateau. The distance was too great to make out detail. Quillen turned.

The rider was closer now. Quillen saw that the man's horse had been hard ridden. The rider slumped in the saddle, his body swaying easily with the motion of the lope. As he neared Quillen, he pulled the animal to a walk and approached watchfully. It paid to be wary in the plains country in this year 1867. With the war two years past and the South gripped in the fist of Yankee reconstruction, law and order were words only.

Quillen smiled. He pulled off the black hat and wiped his face on a coat sleeve. The rider halted ten paces away and stared coldly. A rifle lay across his thighs.

"Had to shoot my horse," Quillen offered. "You going in to town?"

The rider said nothing. His eyes surveyed the scene and returned to Coy. An expression of distaste twisted his dust-caked face.

Except for the black, flat-crowned hat, Coy Quillen wore the field uniform of a Federal Artilleryman. Red noncom stripes down each blue trouser leg, faint marks on coat sleeves where chevrons had been. And a pistol belted high on the right side. The Navy Colt he'd once been so proficient with.

"The war's over, friend," he said to the horseman.

"Not around here, bluebelly. Not around here it ain't." He kneed his mount until the clean-metal mouth of the rifle bore on Quillen's chest.

"You're wrong," Quillen said. He took a step toward the man.

"Hold it right there! You're close enough. I got to look at you. I ain't got to smell you."

The man's hostility grated on Quillen. He narrowed his eyes, fought down growing irritation. His wide shoulders lifted and then slumped.

"All right," he said. "I don't want no trouble. I'll get to town best way I can."

He turned away. And as he did he saw the brand on the horse's lathered hip. He stopped, turned back to face the rider.

"That's my iron," he said. "Your horse, there. Q-P connected." He smiled tentatively. "I'm Coy Quillen."

The pale-eyed rider shifted his grip on the rifle and for a moment Quillen thought he would shoot. The dust-streaked face showed nothing. Finally the man spoke.

"Say that again."

"I said it. I'm Coy Quillen."

"Coy Quillen," Pale-eyes said. "Well, I'll be damned. You made a mistake, Quillen. Coming back to Two Trees. Folks around here heard you got killed at Gettysburg. Most allowed it was a good thing." The man's caked lips curled derisively. "Yeah, I heard all about you. The turncoat—man with principles."

Quillen kept his eyes on the man, plucked idly at the stripes on his leg.

"A man fights," he said. "Sometimes for what he believes in."

"You're a turncoat sonofabitch!" the rider spat, suddenly vicious.

"Don't say that again ..."

The rifle moved slightly and Quillen heard the hammer snick back.

"I'll say it. I'll say what I like and you'll listen. You should have stayed away, Quillen."

"I got no quarrel with you. I'm home, and I'm staying. The war's over."

The rider grinned. He straightened in the saddle and spun the rifle easily in one sun-browned hand. He poked it into the scabbard and socked it home.

"Over, huh? You might change your mind about that. You just might."

Quillen kept his voice even. "I won't change. For five years I've been planning about coming back to Kewpie. Dreaming about it. To Two Trees, people I used to know."

"Used to know?" The man hawked and spat, the wet landing by Quillen's boot. "That's what you'll get from 'em. Can you take that, Quillen?"

After a moment, a long moment, Coy nodded. He turned away from the rider. "I can take it." He looked out over the lifeless plain. "I fought for the Union because I believed in what they fought for. You don't understand that. All right. That's fine. Folks don't like what I did, well, that's too bad."

"They won't."

"Then I'll rub their faces in it." He looked up at the pale-eyed man. "That goes for loud-mouthed punchers, too."

The rider tensed, moved a hand to the rifle stock protruding from the saddle scabbard. Then he kneed his horse toward Quillen, pushed back his hat and leaned down from the saddle. His eyes were so blue they seemed to be no color at all. There was a red line where the hat had rested just below a smooth sweep of hair so pale it was almost white. The eyes were cold, like milkish-blue oysters.

"Here's something to think about on the long walk to town. Your daddy's dead. The South is whipped. Good and whipped. The only government in this country's wearing clothes just like yours." He straightened, smirking. "You're gonna be real popular, Quillen. Yes, sir, Mr. Kewpie—you're gonna be real popular."

He pulled the horse around.

"And I wouldn't be figuring too hard on running Kewpie," he said. "Your brother, Bud, tried that when the Second Texas turned him loose. He wound up talkin' to himself."

The horse danced. "Wait," Coy said. "What did you mean by that? What happened to Bud? Isn't Anse Prinell running Kewpie?"

"Don't worry about your brother. He's in town. You'll see him. If he don't shoot you."

The man laughed.

"And Anse Prinell? You know the Prinells?"

"I know 'em."

"My father's partner. Why would Kewpie be in trouble if Anse is around? I just don't believe things're all as bad as you say, fella."

"Believe what you like," the rider said curtly. He gathered the reins.

"Just a minute there…" Coy looked the man over carefully and obviously. He would want to remember this man. "You've been mighty helpful, mister. Mind telling me your name?"

"Not at all. My name's Maddux," the pale-eyed gunman said. "Harley Maddux. You'll be hearin' it."

He wheeled the pony and lifted it into a dead run down the slope toward town. Quillen stared after him. His jaw was tight and his clothes clung to his body. He reached up, pushed the black hat far back on his head.

"Home," he said, and stared uncertainly through the golden waves of heat toward Two Trees.

CHAPTER 2

T HE DUSTY ROAD behind him stretched out endlessly empty. He looked down at the dead horse. Blood and dust. He'd seen enough killing. The horse had carried him far and faithfully. Here the horse had died.

"Along with a dream," he said aloud.

Then he shook himself and thought for the hundredth time that he'd better get over the habit of speaking aloud to himself. People wouldn't understand. In the roar of artillery warfare, it had served to keep him sane.

Stooping to the swelling animal, he slipped the saddle and bags free, pulled the bridle over the dusty ears. The head flopped and stirred a puff of dust. All this was done with one hand, the left. The other he held cuddled against his body. He straightened and dropped the sweat-stained hull and mopped his face. It was hot. Texas hot. He pushed at the hat with the bad right hand.

He looked at it. A perpetual half-closed fist. The fingers were broad and strong looking, but bent inward toward the palm. They moved not at all.

A fleshy claw.

The hand appeared normal from the back. Broad, like the rest of the man, and deeply tanned; the wrist thick and sturdy, connecting an arm corded with muscle. But the palm showed damage. It was a mass of corrugated ridges; serried white scar tissue mounting from the heel to the pad-fat of the fingers.

He rubbed the ridges, muttered, "Might as well get on."

He kicked the saddle and bags under a convenient clump of the tough plain's grass. The Henry rifle he'd bought in St. Louis he pulled from the scabbard. He'd better carry the weapon. Repeaters were still enough of a novelty to be coveted on the frontier. Then he started down the long slope, a big figure, thick at chest and shoulders, bulky-thighed and long in the legs; striding free and easy like a man who has walked his share.

In an hour he had reached the dry wash just south of where Two Trees' main street began. The sun was still high in the cloudless bowl above. Quillen stood, resting a moment, gazing ahead at the town he had left almost six years before—to fight against the Confederacy.

A rider passed him at a trot. The cowboy, a young one Coy didn't recognize, glanced at him suspiciously as he wheeled the short-coupled cow pony past. Quillen looked after him, trying to read the horse's brand. He could not.

He stood for a moment, trying to beat some of the accumulated dust from his clothing. His hat resisted brushing; he beat it against his boots. Then he walked slowly up the surprisingly long length of a Main Street he no longer knew.

Sod and 'dobe had given way to brick and board. Even the smell—settling dust, sweaty leather, and the acrid odor of horse—was overpowered by a tang of progress; new wood and hot tar. Four of the new buildings were saloons. That was a surprise, too. Two Trees wasn't a saloon town. Or hadn't been. One, a twostoried board building, had pre-empted the choice location where the Grange Hall had stood. The sign said *Drover's Rest.* Coy's father had built the Grange Hall. It had been a point of pride to the owner of the sprawling and vigorous Kewpie. He and Anse Prinell had given the building to Case County and the people of Two Trees as a gesture of friendship in a time when the small ranchers and dirt scrabblers had been of a mind to make trouble for the local colossus. Now it was no more; replaced by this palace of pleasure.

Quillen stopped in front of the raw-wood building and considered the establishment. A ragged group of loungers on the high board porch considered him in return. He ignored the hostile looks, the low muttering.

The Drover's Rest was quite a place. Music, tinny and inexpert, drifted under the push-type half-doors. From the level of the street Quillen could see under the doors to the room beyond. It was big. And surprisingly full of people. For an afternoon. A bray of laughter poured out into the dusty sunlight, obscene in the clean heat of day.

"Renegade!"

The word echoed. Before Quillen could pull his eyes from the saloon interior, one of the porch-squatters spat from his elevated position. The gob flew a scant inch from Coy's boot. He looked down.

"Second time today," he said soberly. "Local custom?"

His head came up, slowly, eyes searching. One man shifted uneasily under Quillen's stare, leaned back from his perch on the wooden rail. He was a stocky man, bearded and bold-eyed, wearing a floppy Confederate campaign hat and filthy gray trousers. His belt held a gun.

"You came pretty close to my boot, there, friend," Coy said evenly. "It was an accident—wasn't it?"

He stared straight at the man as he advanced to the steps. The offender looked to the loafers with him on the porch. No one moved. All watched Quillen. The stocky man scrambled away from the rail, gripped his weapon without drawing.

"Get on back where you belong, turncoat!" He pushed at the others to make room. Then he stood ready, waiting for Coy to mount the steps. "We don't need you now. Get on back to your Yankee friends!"

Coy kept coming, not hurrying. The man fell back a step. Then, seeing no way out except over Quillen, he rushed forward, mouthing curses.

Someone yelled, "Kill the sonofabitch, Chub!"

The man kicked out viciously at Quillen's face. Coy watched the swinging foot, the roweled boot, coming at him. He was calm. No anger moved him. At the last second he crouched and took the kick on his right shoulder, caught the spur and flipped.

He heaved as the stocky man lunged and the momentum carried the spitter over Quillen's shoulder to land heavily in the hard-packed dirt of the street.

"Get up, Chub," an excited voice called.

Quillen turned.

"Well, let's give him a hand," another offered.

"Wait!" A slim, easy-smiling cowboy appeared, held up a hand. "Chub's fight. He's got a chance comin'. If he's able to take it. Let 'em alone."

Coy laughed and nodded to the puncher, stepped lightly to the street. Chub, struggling to arise from the dust, looked up. Quillen was on him. The stocky man pulled his pistol, started to raise it. Coy brushed the weapon aside, sledged the man behind the ear with a whistling left hand like a pole maul. Chub grunted and buried his face in the powdery dust. The watchers groaned.

Quillen turned. The men had crowded to the rail. The slim puncher stepped forward. He wore a tattered leather vest and one very deadly looking gun tied down to the thigh. A reckless smile twisted his face. He was very young.

"Can't let a renegade get away with that," he said, "now, can we? Somebody hold my hat."

"Get him, Davey!"

"Let's all get him!"

They crowded the rail, started down the steps.

"Run the bastard back to Washin'ton …"

"Hold it!" a voice cried ringingly.

Quillen glanced over his shoulder. A soldier walked from the other sidewalk, striding importantly, hand upraised. An officer, Quillen saw. A captain of United States cavalry according to the crossed sabers on the collar of his rumpled field coat. He wore a forage cap tipped forward, shading a petulant face dominated by black mustaches protruding from a wide and pale upper lip. A big, redheaded sergeant, bright chevrons shining in the sun, followed the chunky captain. He carried a carbine at the ready.

"What's going on here?" The captain puffed, halting beside Quillen. He peered upward. "You traveling through, Trooper?"

A man called from the porch, "Mind your own knitting, you bluebellied crook!"

The captain stiffened. His fat stomach trembled. He pulled a dragoon pistol from his belt holster and pointed it deliberately and carefully at the jeering crowd.

"Silence!" he shouted. "Silence, I say." A little of the noise died. "Sergeant! Shoot the next man that speaks. That's an order."

"Just a minute, Captain," Quillen said. "We got no trouble we can't handle. Put up your gun."

"These men were going to jump you. I saw it."

"And I was fixing to make 'em unjump me, Captain."

"Oh, a tough one. Are you trying to tell me my business?" His eyes searched Quillen's sleeves. "Sergeant? Or is it private?"

"Civilian. I was discharged five months ago."

"Sign him up, De Puys," the slim puncher offered easily. "He'll make a dandy for your renegade crew."

"Be still, Forrestor," the officer said, moving the blue mouth of his weapon to cover the man. "I'm aware of you and your group. You make trouble—any trouble at all—and I'll blow your head off and toast your death before you strike the ground."

Forrestor smiled insolently, said nothing. Quillen shifted in the dust. He edged away from the captain. This was all he needed; being protected by Union troops. He scowled at the officer, stepped farther away.

"Obliged," he said. "But I reckon I'll take care of any trouble I contact myself."

"Just a moment there. What's your name? What outfit were you discharged from? Cover him, too, Sergeant."

The grizzled noncom moved the carbine a hair. The muzzle drifted toward Quillen. The sergeant's face, sun-reddened and wind-whipped, reflected his opinion of the affair. He shrugged, winked at Quillen over the captain's shoulder.

"I asked you a question, fellow."

"Sergeant," Quillen said stiffly. "Fifth United States Artillery."

"Fifth, huh? Charley Griffin's Corps. Who commanded your company? Where were you discharged? How come you waited almost two years after the war ended to get out? Get in trouble? Court martial?"

"Which one of them questions you want me to answer, Captain?"

"Never mind. What's your business in Two Trees?"

"Look here," Coy said, "I don't see what..."

"Just answer the question, Sergeant."

"Why," Quillen said, drawing it out, "I live here, Captain. I was born here."

The officer reddened; he waved his pistol toward the whooping crowd. Now they all laughed, slapping thighs and pointing at the hopping mad little cavalryman in the street. One of the roughs, under cover of the general mirth, pulled a pistol, thrust it through the tangle of arms. Quillen saw the blue gleam and started to cry out. There was no need. The big sergeant had seen, also. He flicked the carbine almost casually, pulled the trigger.

A man fell in the crowd, boot heel disintegrated by the force of the fifty-caliber ball. The group stilled abruptly.

The sergeant flipped out his pistol, spoke shortly: "Fun's all right. We ain't having no. gunplay. Put it away or eat some o' this."

The fallen man looked up, mumbled into his collar. But he replaced the weapon in its holster. The little captain's face was pulled out of shape, mottled strangely. He faced the mob, body trembling, lips tight with humiliation.

Not afraid, Quillen thought. The gun in his pudgy fist was steady as a rock. Mad, but not afraid at all. And when the officer spoke, the bluster was gone, replaced by firm command.

"You men," he barked. "Stand where you are. Another outburst of this nature and you'll find yourselves weaponless within the limits of town. I know you resent our presence. I know you would like to see the Union Army leave Texas, leave the South. But that's not possible so we'll both have to make the best of the situation."

"Why ain't it possible?" Forrestor asked.

"Because men without principle ravage this land, milk the resources of a conquered people," De Puys retorted.

"Hoo, hah!"

"Yeah, men like you," a voice from the rear called.

"And Matt Conroy," another shouted.

All of the men began muttering at that. A crowd had gathered behind and they, too, joined the general murmur.

De Puys glanced around. "Silence!" he screamed.

Quillen moved a few steps away and stood ready. Anything could happen here. The scene was explosive and he was now only incidental to it. Deeper issues than hazing a renegade were at odds here.

"We been silent long enough," Forrestor said. He turned. "What's that name you called?"

"Matt Conroy!" someone yelled and then it was taken up by several.

"Matt Conroy!" they chorused.

There was a rustle in the crowd. The men fell away, revealing the doorway of the Drover's Rest. A slender man, almost impossibly elegant in a broadcloth suit and flowered vest, stood there before the gently swinging doors. His face was impassive. From a slim cigar clenched between tiny white teeth thin smoke curled upward. He stepped forward and the ragged punchers fell away. The muttering died. At the edge of the porch the dapper man halted, looked around slowly. His eyes hit on Quillen, paused almost imperceptibly, then went on. He removed the cigar, smiled thinly.

"Somebody call me?" The elegant man turned on splendid small boots and sent a full smile into the crowd behind him. "I thought I heard my name. No? A man can be mistaken."

Quillen watched this man carefully. Something plucked at his soldier's instinct, made him wary. He snorted, impatient with the trend of his thoughts. He didn't even know this little man. But there was something deadly in one unarmed man facing down a crowd. A Texas crowd.

Conroy turned back to the officer. "Afternoon, Captain." He gestured with the cigar. "Rather warm to be pointing guns at people, wouldn't you say? Or perhaps, Captain, you intended something different—like shooting someone? Someone who doesn't believe in the Federal Army running Texas."

"I'll drop him, sir, if you give the word," the redheaded sergeant muttered, not moving his lips.

Quillen heard, there in the street, but the words were not loud enough to reach Conroy. The captain silenced his noncom with a gesture. He holstered his own weapon.

"Not at all, Conroy. We stopped these roughs from misusing a veteran. We will continue to act in whatever manner seems appropriate within the scope of military expediency. Without regard for your wishes, I might add."

"Indeed? And what of this man?"

Quillen stepped forward. He looked directly into Conroy's eyes. They were brown, soft—open but at the same time secretive. Coy stopped on the bottom step, looked up.

"Little trouble," he said. "Personal. The captain had no call to get involved. And neither have you, mister. Now if you'll step aside, I'll go on in there like I intended and cut some Texas dust."

For a moment the smile slipped from Conroy's lips. Then he moved back, spread an inviting palm toward the door behind him.

"Of course, Mr. Quillen."

Coy stopped, one foot raised. No one had mentioned his name. He drew a slow breath.

"You know me, I see."

"Oh, yes. You see, big fella, I've been expecting you. You'll have your first drink in Two Trees with me. On the house. I'm Matt Conroy."

"Yeah. I gathered that." Quillen moved up to the man, looked down at him. "About the drink, I don't know. You, now—you know a man named Maddux? Harley Maddux?"

"Certainly. He works for me. Now come have that drink. You and I have much to discuss."

A man in the crowd laughed abruptly. Conroy whirled. The sound ceased.

"One more thing," Quillen said, not moving. "Where's Anse Prinell?"

Conroy turned easily, face bland once more. "He's dead. Now, like I said, let's go have that drink."

CHAPTER 3

QUILLEN came awake all at once. As an old soldier should; as any soldier had better if he wishes to become an old soldier. The room was completely alien. And dark. He shook his head, immediately regretted it. It throbbed heavily. He lifted a hand and rubbed his face, slowly, not jarring. His mouth tasted bad, like a gun team had stabled there overnight. Why did his head hurt? There must have been whisky. Lots of whisky. His memory was soft, edgy.

He looked for a square of light that would mean a window, but the surrounding darkness was unrelieved. He blinked and groaned softly. He was not a drinking man. Momentarily he expected to hear the morning bugle and the myriad sounds of a gun park coming awake. And then he remembered.

This was Two Trees. He struggled upright on the narrow bed. Giddiness almost claimed him, but he shrugged it off with an effort of will. There was something he had to remember—something about Kewpie.

It came back then. All of it. The events of the afternoon and evening since his return rushed through his mind, without order, clear as living it again. Uncle Anse dead. Kewpie gone. And Lydia . . . and the little man, Matt Conroy.

The Drover's Rest had been a revelation to Coy Quillen. He had followed Conroy into the place for the drink they were to have. He was amazed. The bar was large. Much larger than the brief glimpse from the street had indicated. Along the left-hand wall ran a magnificent bar of a dark wood like mahogany. Behind this thick wood columns bracketed scrolled mirrors of incredible brightness and clarity. For the drinking wants of the scattered punchers, off-duty troopers, and troupe of giggling girls, four white-coated barmen worked quietly and expertly behind the impressive plank. A few of the drinkers were men Quillen knew. Had known, he amended silently. They all looked away as his eyes touched them.

Conroy walked through the room quickly while Coy dawdled, surveying this unexpected oasis. A profusion of hanging candle-wheels, now unlit, dotted the low ceiling. Tables and chairs, good finished furniture, filled the central portion directly in front of the entrance. In the rear, under a full-length balcony, a bevy of gambling sets were getting desultory play. Faro layouts, complete with high-sitting gun guards; poker tables, green-covered and round; a gigantic Big Six wheel, gilded spokes flashing.

Quillen searched for Conroy. He had lost the dapper man in the confusion. Then he saw him. At the street end of the bar. Conroy nodded, motioned. Quillen moved uneasily through the room.

Conroy turned from the bar, greeted him. "Well, Quillen. What do you think?"

"I was in St. Louis a while back. Even there this would be fine."

He pushed a boot on the metal rail. Smooth—brass, maybe. He turned to the little man, eyed him with distaste. Conroy still smiled. He waved his cheroot, smile deepening under Quillen's scrutiny.

"Order what you like."

"Whisky."

"Coffee," Conroy told the barman. There was a small silence. Then he said, "Quillen, I've a rather sad duty to perform. Since I'm a man who never takes a chance, I'll tell you first about the man directly behind you."

Coy turned his head, then came all the way around. The man was huge. Not tall, but big in every other way. He bulked a good two inches under Quillen's own six feet. Bunchy muscles pushed at an ill-fitting suit, red wrists dangled inches out of the sleeves. His hands were wide and scarred. Quillen recognized him immediately. A type he had become thoroughly familiar with in the course of training wartime recruits. This was a plug-ugly. A docker. Vicious, amoral hulks from the wharf areas of New York and other large eastern cities. Snarling and contemptuous they were; living only because they had become more strong, more adept at violence, than their fellows.

Quillen stared. He couldn't help it. The man looked at him in return, his face utterly devoid of expression. The eyes were pinheads deeply buried behind thick frontal bone and bushy brows. Hair grew far down on the scarred forehead and the man measured no more than a quarter-inch between the eyes. Coy had never seen a more torn visage, a face so twisted and hammered by fists as to have almost no area of whole skin. A small whistle came as the man's breath forced its way through an absolutely flattened nose.

Conroy's voice came over his shoulder.

"That's Moriarty," he said and Quillen turned back to the bar, gripped the drink before him. "He is my man," Conroy went on. "I mean just that. Mine. But then you will come to know that I mean what I say always. I never imply or infer. I tell you now that I show you Moriarty to insure my personal safety." He smiled, lifted his coffee. "You have the look of an imprudent man, Quillen. I wouldn't want you to hurt me."

Quillen gaped. Nothing in his life had equipped him for a man like this. He downed his drink with a quick jerk of his left hand. Conroy's eyes followed the action, traveled to the hanging right hand. He smiled.

"But then," he said, "perhaps I needn't have worried. I see you have a bad hand."

"You're very observing."

"Yes. A memento of the war, no doubt?"

"Never mind the hand. What's your business with me?"

Conroy stroked his neat mustache with his little finger, flicked his eyes to the gun hanging at Quillen's right hip, butt pointed back. Coy reached around with his left hand, pulled the Colt free. He laid the weapon on the bar.

"Take a look," he said. "Don't break your neck; just go ahead and look."

"There's not much chance of our becoming friendly, is there?" the little man said, his eyes moving from the gun to Quillen.

"No. So ..."

"Of course, not you, big fella." Conroy sipped his coffee. His eyes slitted, fixed on Coy's reflection in the mirror. "Coy Quillen," he said musingly. "You know, I never expected to see you. I knew about you. When I came to this country, I made it my business to find out about everyone connected with Kewpie. You and your brother were off to war. You, on the wrong side."

"Get to it, Conroy," Quillen blurted. "If you've got something to say, say it." He replaced the gun in its holster.

"Now there's no real hurry. You're my guest. Have another drink." He signaled the bartender. "What happened to your hand?"

"What happened to Anse Prinell?"

Conroy turned. The smile fled and the brown eyes grew murky. He leaned negligently against the bar and looked at Coy.

"I told you," he said. "He's dead. And before you hear it somewhere else—folks think I did it. They're wrong."

"If you did," Quillen said as unemotionally as the other had spoken, "you're a dead man." His curved hand hung at the holster flap.

"Don't be a fool. Moriarty will crack your skull before you clear leather. A dozen men in this room would shoot you if I winked."

"Probably." Coy took a breath, held it. His thighs hurt from clenching. "But one thing you'd better know. If you killed Anse Prinell," he said, flat, cold, "I'll find it out. And nothing in the world will save you."

"You're a talker, I see." The small man shrugged, swished his coffee around in the cup. "That's as may be."

"How did it happen?"

"Line camp. Two riders found him. Shot in the back. From long range with a small-bore." He looked up, set the cup down on the bar. "I'll tell you once more. I didn't do it."

"When?"

"Two months ago. Immediately everyone said I was responsible. I don't mind that. I'm a businessman, Quillen. I came to this wilderness from New York to make a fortune. And that's what I'm going to do. If someone gets caught in my machinery, I'm sorry." The smile crept back. "That's not a threat. I didn't kill Anse Prinell."

"Why were you blamed? Why? I'd like to know that."

Conroy flipped the ash from his cigar with a deliberate movement. He looked down. "Because I bought the Q-P connected. Kewpie."

The words were clear enough. They just didn't mean anything. Not to Quillen. It was as if someone had said the sun would no longer shine. Ever. His mind refused it for one blank moment. Then the import sank in and he half raised a hand in protest.

"You bought Kewpie? But you couldn't. It's mine and Bud's."

"I did. And it's legal. Now, don't get wild ..."

"Listen, Conroy," Coy said. "When my father died a letter came to me from Paul Angelarry, father's lawyer. He said his share—my father's share—went to Bud and me."

Conroy turned away. He nodded to the barman who stepped forward with fresh coffee. He also refilled Quillen's glass.

"I bought it," Conroy said, sipping the black brew, "from the government."

"The government?"

"That's right. Fifth Military District, represented in the transaction by a Federal judge. So it's legal, big fella. Kewpie commands the plateau. And it has all of the solid water—water that everyone in the area needs."

"You're a snake, Conroy."

The man shrugged. "A businessman."

Coy gripped his glass, drained it with a quick motion. He set the glass down, turned to Matt Conroy. "So it's legal, is it?"

"You might ask your brother that, Quillen."

"Bud? Why?"

"He foolishly decided that I had no right to buy Kewpie out from under him. He thought you were dead, you see. And Kewpie was his and the Prinell woman's as far as we knew. He tried to fight. Claimed persecution because he had been a Johnny Reb."

"What happened?" Quillen's throat was tight. He stepped closer to the dapper man. "What happened?"

"Stop jumping to conclusions. Your kid brother is all right. The cavalry dispossessed him. Along with the Prinell women-folks. That's all."

"The cavalry? That funny little captain?"

"You're calmer, I see. That's fine. After all, it's just business. Have another drink."

Quillen got his glass off the bar without taking his eyes from Conroy. He swallowed the fiery stuff and it tasted like water.

"That's better," Matt Conroy said. "Now I'll tell you. We had an order from Judge Holman of this district. Piece of paper. Little thing. Notice to yield under law. Ah, learning—wonderful thing." He studied the dregs in his cup, his lip quirked.

"I can't believe it," Quillen said. "I can't believe it from you. But I'll find out. I aim to find out a lot of things."

"Find away," Conroy said airily. "Believe what you like. It's true. All of it. See your lawyer."

"I'll do that."

"Fine. Now you know why I was suspected when Prinell got—when he died. Now get out. You tire me, Quillen. I've said what I wanted to say."

"Well, I don't think I've said all mine now," Coy said slowly. "You, uh—you have any idea who killed Anse Prinell?"

"Look, big fella. I've done nothing outside the law. Nothing. I owe you nothing. Not even explanations. So don't try my patience. Don't give me any trouble and we'll get along."

Quillen stood away from the bar—stood tall. His shoulder hunched slightly. "Trouble," he said—and somehow it came out easy. "Mister, you don't know what trouble is. But you'll find out ..."

Quillen's voice scaled off, hot finally, the anger showing. Conroy just smiled. He slumped against the bar, fingering the tiny gold knife hung on his fancy vest.

"Will I?" The smile widened until the tiny teeth showed white against his skin. "I won't enjoy fighting a cripple. But suit yourself."

"You'll get trouble," Coy said, moving forward. He struggled to control himself. Moriarty stood behind him, slightly to the right, a hulking presence. "But I'll use the same kind of weapons. Legal trouble, Conroy. That's the kind I believe in."

"Is that so?"

"Yes. You're damn right, that's so. I'm not a vanquished Confederate. I can appeal to Sheridan—and be heard. You're all right with the law? Fine. Then I'll fight you legal. So goddam legal it'll turn up your toes!"

The room quieted. Footsteps rattled by on the porch, rapping. A nervous croupier dropped a handful of chips.

"You haven't a friend in the county, big fella," Conroy said. "Remember that."

"I'll remember. Tomorrow I'm heading for Tracy. We'll see what an examiner from the Land Commissioner's office thinks about it. We'll damn soon find out how legal it is."

Conroy picked up his cup, looked at Quillen over the porcelain rim.

"Land Commissioner," he said and shook his head sadly.

Quillen turned away from the man, downed a drink. His knuckles tapped on the smooth leather of the holster at his side.

"I had hoped," Conroy said, "that we could work something out."

"Like what?"

"I don't know. You can't hurt me, you can't get Kewpie back. Seems to me your position is real bad. Making trouble won't help. Be a lot better if you let things alone."

"Yes," Coy said, "I guess it would. For you." He turned, stepped toward the door. "Thanks for the drink."

"Quillen," Conroy said and Coy stopped. "Aren't you curious about Mrs. Prinell? And her daughter? I thought the Q and the P stuck together."

Coy's face stiffened. "They do," he said softly. "It's always been Quillen and Prinell."

Conroy said, "Anse Prinell's widow is staying with the Morlys. Doctor Morly."

Quillen's eyes half closed. He moved back to the bar, stepping carefully.

"Go on," he said tightly.

"Go on? Oh, yes. You mean the tender and exciting Lydia. You and she were quite—how shall I say it?"

"Don't say it at all. Just tell me where she is."

"Here," Conroy said, not smiling any longer. "Upstairs, to be exact."

Coy tensed. He felt his knees bending, back tightening. Conroy's eyes moved to Moriarty, still standing slightly behind Quillen.

"She's my woman," Conroy said.

Down the bar someone dropped a glass and it rolled and rolled. A door slammed far off. Quillen didn't move. His eyes almost closed and he lifted his head oddly, expectantly.

"What makes you think I care?" His lips barely moved. Moriarty sidled close and Quillen was aware of him by some queer splitting of his consciousness. Conroy just smiled.

"Your woman, you say." Coy shifted his weight. "Your woman."

Quillen knew he would die if he tried to fumble the pistol from the holster hanging uselessly at his right hand. And he had never wanted more to take a life than at this moment. The right hand twitched and Conroy laughed aloud.

"I learned something today," Quillen said, the words barely audible.

He spat suddenly into his left hand. Whisky spit, green as bile, cupped in a horny palm. Then he wiped the palm from forehead to chin in the face of the laughing man.

Spittle hung on Conroy's nose and chin. He froze. His face drained of blood and the pretty mustache stood out against the sudden pallor; the brown eyes became colorless with fury.

"Moriarty!" he screamed. His throat vibrated with it.

Quillen pivoted and flung himself aside, lashing out with his fists. He was not quick enough. His knuckles met air and a stunning crash on his head limbered his legs. Thoughts pinwheeled. Through a red haze he saw a thick arm raised above him. It came down and the blow was painless.

In the stifling closeness of the strange room, Quillen sat and re-lived that painful moment. But the time for anger had passed.

"Kewpie, gone..." he muttered.

He remembered the night, on his sixteenth birthday it had been, when his father took him for a ride across Kewpie. Sam Quillen, normally a hard-working, uncommunicative man, opened up that night.

"All a man needs, Coy," he said, his tough old voice rasping in the soft dark, "is right here. Kewpie will sustain me and mine, you and yours, as long as grass will grow. It's enough." He had looked deeply into his son's young eyes. "Hear me, boy? Enough for any man to live for. And, if need be, to die for ..."

He cursed the remembrance there in the airless room. And as he did the hopeless feeling left him and his mighty frame, rock-hard and powerful from years of wrestling mired caisson wheels and swinging field-piece trails by hand, responded to returning juices. He touched his head. Pain rang like struck iron.

"Mr. Moriarty," he said grimly.

The sound of his voice was startling in the still room and he realized that no other sound came to him at all. It was quiet, like a line camp in the dead of winter. He felt himself in the darkness. Nothing broken and no pain save for the knot buried in his wiry hair. His clothes were still on his body. Dusty and evil-smelling now. His nose wrinkled. The room smelled bad, too. There had to be a window. He searched his pockets for a match and noticed then that his gunbelt had been removed. He reached out beside the bed and touched a chair, fumbled on it. No gun.

At that moment there was a sound. A metallic click. Coy tensed, gathered his weight under him. A latch snicked and a yellow crack appeared in the solid black. A door. Right in front of him. It was opening. He moved on the bed and the treacherous mattress crackled with the shift.

"Coy?" a voice asked. A woman's voice. "Coy, are you awake?" It came through the door in a guarded whisper.

The door opened. For a moment Quillen's sight was killed by the lamplight streaming through.

"Who is it? Who's there?"

The figure, limned by the light of a tall lamp carried in one hand, advanced into the room. There was a dry rustle of skirts and a sharp, clean odor reached Quillen's nostrils.

"Who is it?" he asked again.

But he knew. Oh, he knew, all right ...

"It's Lydia," the girl said, a little breathless. "Who were you expecting, darling?"

CHAPTER 4

S HE STOOD smiling down at him. A tall woman, slender and willowy with that strange suggestion of strength some beautiful women have. Her hair was piled high, leaving delicate ears free. Her lips were full and moist-appearing in the lamplight.

Coy Quillen stared. It had been so long. He wanted to say something; take her in his arms. But the words of Matt Conroy echoed in his head. His throat moved, but no words came. There were too many things to say—too many years between them. Between what they had had together and now.

"Well," Lydia said, feeling the strangeness, too. "Aren't you going to ask me to sit down, or something?"

She placed the lamp on a rough table near the bed.

"Lydia," he said, and it tasted good. So many times. So very many. "You shouldn't be here."

She laughed, perched on the bed near him.

"Do you know where you are, then?"

Her odor came to him, sharp and clean—cool, like early morning and freshly washed linen.

"Wherever it is, you shouldn't be here. Now. With me."

He moved away. The light showed a window across the room. It was tightly curtained. He walked to it, swaying slightly, tore aside the curtains and opened the sash a few inches. Night air spilled into the fetid atmosphere of the room.

"Yes, it was a little warm in here," the girl said. There was strain in her voice.

Quillen looked at her, lovely in the lamplight. His stomach fluttered. He turned to the window. It overlooked a stable and corral area. He craned his neck, but could recognize no landmark. He turned.

"Drover's Rest," she said. Her eyes found his for a second and then she looked away. "This is the back room, upstairs. Sometimes Matt's—Mr. Conroy's men stay here."

"Yes," he said. "You would know, I suppose."

The girl caught the surge of bitterness in his tone. She sighed, looked at her hands.

"Are you judging me, Coy?"

He walked to her on stiff legs, loomed over her.

"Shouldn't I? Weren't you promised to me?" She said nothing; neither moved. "Is it true, what Conroy told me? Are you ... is ..."

"That we live here together?" She lifted her chin, eyes wide. "That I'm his woman? Is that what he told you?"

"It's true," he said, knowing that he'd accepted it all along.

"Yes," she said evenly. "As far as it goes—it's true. All of it."

"Then what can I say? I didn't believe him. Today. In the—in the place. I would never believe it, except ..."

"Except from my lips ... my lying lips!"

He nodded. There was a pain in him, aside from the bruises.

The girl stood, faced him. Her eyes, gray he remembered though the light was not sufficient to tell, bore into his. Her lips trembled a trifle, the only evidence of emotion.

"What was I to do, Coy? Tell me that and I'll understand. You left us," she accused. "You left and Uncle Sam died and there was only father. He tried after your father died. But Sam Quillen was always the strength of Kewpie. Anse Prinell tried—but you left us, Coy. You left us alone."

"You know why I left." He looked away from the girl. "I believed in this country. More than anything—like Sam taught me. But I believed in its advancement. Its destiny. I still do. But I couldn't believe in an isolated Confederacy of renegade states, dedicated to stagnation and the preservation of all that was old and evil in my eyes."

"You needn't make your speech, Coy. I've heard it many times. Remember?"

"It was the method I objected to," he went on, as if she hadn't spoken. "I did what I had to do, Lydia. Anarchism, hiding behind a mask of old-world manners. Well, this isn't an old world! And it doesn't fit. It's new, and—and vigilant and made for *all* people. I believed…"

"I know what you believed." The girl's voice softened. "'Old Law 'n Order.' That's what we called you, Bud and I. Your biggest boosters, we were then. 'Do it right and do it regular. Have faith in the orderly processes.'" She smiled up at him. "See? I remember the words."

"Is it a bad way to feel?"

She shook her head. "No, Coy. Not bad. When you left, proud and determined, I loved you for it. Now…"

"Yes," Quillen said, suddenly harsh, wanting to hurt. "Now?"

And the word hung there in the tiny room and accused each of them separately. They'd gone on while others died; time had brought its change.

Quillen's throat felt like a country road in a rainless summer and his head throbbed increasingly. He wanted a drink. But he would not ask the girl. His hand fumbled tobacco from a pocket and a stubby pipe. Filling it, he needn't look at her.

"Well," she said and then the silence seemed twice as loud. After a moment: "Oh, there's no use, I suppose. When it's gone, it's…"

"Yes," he said, biting it off. He stuck the pipe in his mouth, spoke around it. "Never mind. Just let it alone. Do you know everyone thinks your—thinks Conroy killed your father? Did you know that?"

She looked up at him, twisted her hands in her lap. She nodded. Her chin came up.

"I don't suppose it would make any difference if I tried to explain ..."

"Explain?" For a long moment he considered the girl, gaze level, brows drawn together.

"No," he said. "No difference."

Her head dropped. There was a long silence, heavy, uncomfortable. Quillen broke it.

"Tell me how I got here. To this room."

"Conroy," she said. "He had that ape carry you here after the fight. What did you do to him, Coy? I've never seen him like that. He was livid. No one ever reached him like that before."

Quillen smiled for the first time; he looked down at his hand, buffed the palm with bent fingers.

"Why," the girl said, "I believe he hates you, Coy. Really hates you."

"Is that so strange?"

"For Matt Conroy, it is. He says hate is a luxury. That it addles judgment and rapes reason."

"He's right," Quillen said. "And the same goes for love. I'm going to take his counsel. What time is it?"

"Almost dawn. Soon the swamper will be knocking about down below. We must hurry. I came back to get you out."

He swung away from her.

"Am I a prisoner then?"

"I don't know. I really don't. There may be guards down below. I don't know. I came straight here, up the back. I had to wait ..." She blushed suddenly and turned away.

"Till he was asleep," Quillen offered, turning the knife in both of them. "It must be hard—crawling out of bed without waking your playmate."

She bit her lip, hurt flattening the smooth flesh of her face. She stood. Tears appeared in the drawn corners of her eyes. Her fine breasts rose and heaved, pushing outward against the confining dress stuff. She almost ran to the door, turned when she got there.

"You had to do a terrible thing once. You went away and fought against your own people. Because you thought you had to. It was hard, but you went—and you fought."

"Just go," he said, barely audible, wanting her to be gone, the dark beauty shut away.

"No," she said. Her tone became vibrant, intense. "No, I won't go. You fought. With guns, because you were strong and male and able to fight." She wiped a tear carelessly with a flat palm. "I'll tell you this, Coy Quillen—by coming home today, you saved Matt Conroy's life!"

She slammed the door behind her. Coy heard a muffled sob, footsteps running and then silence. He turned blindly to the wall and drew back his arm. He slammed his right hand against the wall and the scar tissue buckled in the ruined palm. Pain rode up on him. It blasted, exploding behind his eyes, and he gathered it to him like a blanket on a cold night.

He walked slowly up the main street of Two Trees. A silent and deserted Two Trees. He had encountered no opposition in leaving the Drover's. Lydia's directions had been exact. He hawked and spat into the street. Lydia.

One light showed in the town, from the corner of Canadian House. The dining-room corner. And that reminded him he hadn't eaten in quite a spell. A pan clattered in the stillness and set a dog to barking. Coy's boots thudded on board. He breathed deeply, chasing whisky fumes and bile with clear morning air.

At the square, where Main Street was crossed and terminated like a giant T by First Street, he paused and gazed upward at the trees. He had thought a lot about this; coming back, visiting the square, the trees.

Symbols, they were. Nature's flaunt in the face of the flat country. Two old trees.

Still there, he mused. Scarred and mightily put upon—but alive. Quillen's earliest recollections were tied up with the gnarled patriarchs from which the town had gotten its name. Two Trees: one, a fearfully old and bowed live-oak, clinging to a life that was at best precarious; the other, a grand pecan, slim branched and serene. They rustled in the morning breeze and talked softly in the manner of trees.

In one swift rush of memory Coy recalled a thousand games of tag and touch-me. He walked to the pecan and laid his palm on the cool bark.

His eyes searched the branches. One, a heavy limb twenty feet from the ground, had a peculiar, symmetrical pattern bisecting it. A worn place. Coy studied the limb idly for a moment, then he remembered. The hanging limb. He pulled his hand away. He wiped it on his uniform coat as he walked away.

The house was clapboard and shingle. A neat stake fence enclosed the yard. A wide walk extended from the street to a broad veranda webbed with creepers and eerie in the half-light. Quillen paused at the gate and peered at the rose-stone walk up which he had stepped so confidently in times past. Long past. He looked for the sign. It was there. It had been there since the beginning of his memory. Somewhat faded and worn, but readable. Coy didn't have to read it to know what the scrolled words said: *Paul Angelarry, Counselor-at-Law.*

He smiled, remembering the many times the fussy, brilliant little man had enjoined him to embrace the law as a career.

"With your mind, Coy," he'd been fond of saying pontifically, "chousing cows is a slap at the Lord that endowed you." Then he would pull meditatively at his muttonchop whiskers. "It is, indeed. The law, now—an honorable and lasting profession. You think it over, boy."

Coy pushed at the gate. It squeaked as the cast-iron counterweight pulled at the ancient rope. At the door of the house he hesitated, no longer sure of his welcome. Yesterday—yes, but today—he shrugged. The lawyer's infrequent letters had been virtually his only link with home during the war years. But still Paul Angelarry was a southerner—a Texas gentleman.

Quillen rubbed his jaw. Stubble on his face. A shave would have helped. Probably he looked like the renegade the roughs named him. He took off the black hat, ran stiff fingers through his hair. Then he knocked loudly on the oak door and waited.

It opened almost immediately. For a cold moment Coy failed to recognize the thin, weary-faced young man standing in the doorway. He was a slightly smaller edition of Coy Quillen; more slender, less rigid of face, less wide of shoulder. He was fully dressed, blinking in the strengthening light.

Coy smiled and stepped forward. "Bud!" he said, voice almost failing. "Bud, it's been ..." He stopped, pushed back the warm words.

Bud Quillen stared at his brother with unmistakable contempt and hostility. Coy recalled that the boy's eyes had always held a repressed sort of deviltry, sparkling with unlaughed laughs; now they were dark with suspicion. Bud Quillen nodded shortly without speaking, stepped aside. Coy moved past him into the house.

"Is this the way it has to be, Bud?" Coy paused in the narrow hall, looked down at the boy. Bud avoided his brother's eyes. He jerked his head in the direction of the kitchen from where light and sound issued.

"Paul's in the kitchen. Eating. He's expecting you." The younger Quillen's voice was flat, restrained, as if in speaking he violated a personal vow.

"Paul? How did he know I was back?"

"The whole town knows," Bud said. "He's been waiting for you. Me, I'd just as leave you'd stayed away."

"You, too? I've been home for less than a day and everyone tells me I should have stayed away. Well, I'm here."

There was a silence. Coy tried to catch his brother's eyes, failed. "I thought we could talk, Bud. We always could in the old days."

"That was then."

"And this is different?"

"Isn't it? You left, that's all. We got nothing to talk about."

"No, that's not all. That's a long way from all."

"You broke Daddy's heart," the boy said. "He always loved you best and when he needed you, you weren't here. No, we got nothing to talk about. Nothing at all."

"A man does what he thinks he must, Bud. At the time. There aren't many second chances. I don't say what I did was right. Or even good. But it was what I thought I had to do. I can't take it back now."

"You betrayed your own, Coy. That's the thing. I don't care who you fought for. That's your business. Principles are fine—I've heard you preach about 'em often enough. But you rode those high-sounding principles into a headstone for Sam Quillen. And that's my business. I ain't forgetting that."

"You make it sound real bad, Buddy."

"Don't call me that!"

"All right," Coy said. He nodded. "Good enough. One thing though. I'm getting Kewpie back. It's Quillen property. No matter what a funny piece of paper says."

"That'll be fine. What the little brother couldn't do, you'll do. That it? Make the county proud of you, huh? Forget you fought for the North. Is that what you want?"

"Bud, what's wrong with you? You never—Look, I'm getting our land back. You want to help?"

Bud Quillen faced his brother in the paneled hallway. He raised bitter eyes and stared deeply into Coy's cold ones.

"No," he said. "And I'll believe it when I see it."

At that moment Paul Angelarry's voice came from the kitchen. Coy hadn't heard the dry, carefully enunciated tones for almost six years, yet he smiled at the words.

"Coy! You think Mother has nothing to do but stand at this stove keeping your vittles warm? Get on in here, boy!"

"Right away, Paul. I'm talking to Bud."

He stopped his brother when he would have passed him in the hallway. Bud's arm was rigid, muscles taut, under Coy's restraining hand.

"Just a minute. Whatever we think personally, we can't let it interfere with getting Kewpie back. If not for us, then for Mrs. Prinell. And for Lydia."

Bud snorted, shook his arm. "Lydia! She's doing all right. She's doing just fine. That girl ain't gonna be no loser."

"Don't say it, Bud."

"You mean you don't know about her? Listen—"

"You listen." Coy towered over the boy; he clamped his teeth to keep from hitting him. "I know, all right. I know all about it. And do you know whose fault it is, Bud? That she's called a tramp and barred from decent homes? Do you know? Well, it's yours. Bud Quillen's—nobody else's."

"You're crazy!"

"Crazy, am I? What did you do about her father's death? How much comfort were you when she lost the only home she'd ever known? How many holes did you put in Anse Prinell's killer?"

Bud's face paled. He raised a palm as if to ward off the accusation. "What could I..." He stopped and his eyes narrowed. "She was your girl. Not mine. You were the one she always ran to. I don't owe her nothing. Nothing!"

"And that absolves you, huh? All right. We got it all straight, now." Coy wheeled, anger riding him, and strode to the kitchen door. He turned. "Keep your tongue off her. That's all. What's done is done. You tell everyone that." His voice dropped to a harsh whisper, filled the small hallway. "First man wags his jaw, why I'll kill him, Bud."

He twisted away and stepped into the orderly, bright kitchen. The warmth hit him in a wave, rich-smelling and homey. It thawed his face and set him to relaxing.

Paul Angelarry, small and neat, huge checkered napkin tucked at his chin covering tie and vest, smiled wryly at Coy's appearance. He shook his head, mutton chops vibrating, eyes suspiciously bright under gray spikes of eyebrow. He turned to his wife at the stove.

"What did I tell you, Mother? Ten minutes in the house and already he's made us accessories to a felony." He rose, extended his hand. "Welcome, boy. Good to have you home. Sit and eat."

Coy grinned as he shook the small, dry hand. His head began bobbing like an embarrassed schoolboy's. The grin widened. The head bobbed. It seemed the damned thing wouldn't ever stop.

He sat. And a long sigh broke from him.

CHAPTER 5

PAUL ANGELARRY was a man of the law, but essentially a pioneer. Food was basic. He would say nothing about Coy's absence, the trouble at home or about Kewpie. Not until Coy had absorbed quantities of breakfast washed down by real coffee, scalding and strong.

Then he said, "All right, Coy. We can't put it off. Let's go to my office."

He led the way out of the kitchen. Coy followed. In the hallway, outside of the residence-office of the peppery little lawyer, he paused. His hand was swollen and red from the mistreatment of the night before. He hefted it in his good hand. How could he fight? He relaxed with an effort and walked into the office.

Paul Angelarry's office was large and light and just a little early-morning chilly. It was a cluttered room, much used, filled with books and files and the mementos of a frontier lifetime. A huge oak desk—Coy had heard many times how Angelarry had had it packed from Santa Fe by wagon and mule—dominated the room and dwarfed the sprightly little man behind it. Angelarry gestured to Quillen who stood, blinking with remembrance, in the doorway.

"Sit down, boy. Sit down," he said. The lawyer bit off a cheroot, lit it quickly. "Not supposed to smoke," he said, glancing at the door. "Gets in the curtains. But—let's get down to issues."

Coy eased his big body into a leather chair. He lit his pipe mechanically and waited for Angelarry to speak. Paul would tell him. But in his own time.

"Coy," the lawyer said through a smoke cloud, "things are much different around here since the war."

"Different everywhere, sir."

"Stop that. You know my name. But you're right—the world is changing. But, nevertheless, more different around here than you can imagine."

"Paul, I know it's been bad. But administrating a defeat is bad, too. Would you think there'd be no abuses?"

"Abuses, you say? Abuses we expect. They are so in use, as Shakespeare aptly put it, that people do but smile." He snorted, blowing out his lips in indignation. "Abuses. Oh, we didn't have it so bad out here during the war. Too far away. But afterward ... Well, for a while the wildness of the country saved us. You know it hasn't been too many years since we chased Kiowas and Comanches as well as cows. But in a way that was bad, not being bothered. We got smug. You remember how it was at first? The Union allowed the Confederate states to draft constitutions, elect representatives, establish and maintain law enforcement agencies. We lived pretty much as we always had. For a little while."

Coy shifted in the big chair. The lawyer's wise old eyes rested on him briefly, then he went on.

"The boys began coming back. Those that were able. Lots didn't make it. Well, that's war. Two of the Gentry boys. You went to school with them. And Ab Forrestor, old Jim Collins's oldest, Elijah ..."

"Forrestor?"

"Yes. The Cross-F. Small outfit. Come to think of it, I guess they showed up after you'd gone. Or about the same time. Alex Forrestor, wife, and four strapping boys."

"I think I met one of them," Quillen said. "He offered to fight me. Tall boy, slim, and kind of reckless looking."

"That'd be Davey. He's a dangerous young man. Even he doesn't know how dangerous. And he has every right to be. But I'll tell you about that later."

Quillen reached to the desk, knocked his pipe against a heavy ash tray. He moved forward on the chair.

"Paul," he said, "tell me about Kewpie."

The old man looked at him and shook his head, the whiskers reflecting sunlight slants angling through the high windows.

"It's gone, Coy. Gone. What you've heard is true. I let 'em steal it, damn my soul!"

"Don't, Paul. Just tell me. I know you did what you could."

"No, Coy. I didn't. If Sam Quillen were alive, he'd take a horsewhip to me. And I'd let him, by Heaven! When they passed that bill—ramrodded it through on a local manifesto, I should have known." He pounded a flat palm on the desk. His dry tone had deserted him. Now he was an angry little man.

"I don't—Paul, I just don't seem to see what you're trying to tell me."

"No. Of course you don't. Why should you? There's never been anything like it. Not in this country. No reason why any fair-thinking man should be expected to grasp it. Here's what happened. Two months ago the Federal government abolished all state constitutions. No more state autonomy for the vanquished confederates. Not even on the puppet level we'd had. They set up a provisional military government of Southern states. Martial law, in effect."

"Drastic situations require drastic measures."

"Perhaps, perhaps. But what followed was inevitable. Five military districts were formed under the command of district supervisors. All general officers. Union, of course. Troops of cavalry were dispatched to key areas. The supervisor appointed military governors with absolute authority."

"That fat little captain." Coy sat up in the chair. Now he began to get an inkling.

Angelarry nodded vigorously and leaned forward over the desk. "Exactly. Captain Peter De Puys. A perfect pig of an officer. And the military governor of Case County."

"I don't see ..."

"Wait, son. This is the happening of two years. Twenty-four hate-filled months. How can I tell you in a word?"

Quillen smiled thinly at the little man and settled back. A vast impatience was building in him. But he realized the lawyer was right; he had to know it all, miss nothing.

"The military moved in," the peppery little man went on. "That was two—almost three months ago." Angelarry sat back, built a tent with his old, dry fingers. He looked at Quillen bleakly from under the spikey brows. "Just before the army, a man came to Two Trees. His name was Matt Conroy."

The name snapped out. Quillen narrowed his eyes. A strange dance of silhouettes performed behind the lids, where only he could see. Lydia. Lydia and Matt Conroy.

Angelarry went on, his eyes fixed on the bright sunlight shafting the window. "This is necessary background, Coy. I'm not just rambling without purpose. Anyway, this man had money. This Conroy. Lots of money. He was ruthless. He bought the Grange Hall and another building and several lots on the town-site. He established saloons. He started with one. Now he has three. He moved real slow, angering no one. He brought in girls. Well, you know how that is. After a while he was well enough established, had enough local people dependent on him, to show his hand."

"That's when he started buying land. He started a sort of company called Land Development Factors. About a year before he'd had a preliminary man in to look over the situation. That was before he, Conroy, came to Two Trees. The man bought every piece of available land around Kewpie. I wondered, but forgot about it. When Conroy started the company, he asked for Kewpie."

Coy sat up abruptly. The lawyer raised a hand.

"I know. You say it was late for wondering and you say correctly. But he was careful, he was smooth—exceedingly circumspect, is Matt Conroy. A very bright man. Make no mistake about that, Coy."

"What happened? With the land, I mean?"

"Well, for a while, nothing. He couldn't buy Kewpie, of course. Anse just laughed at him."

The old man stopped and cleared his throat. Quillen, simmering in his lack of knowledge, sat taut and expectant. But he said nothing.

"Coy, you remember old Charlie Morris? The town marshal?"

"Very well," Coy said. "Used to get him to tie off saddle lacing for me. All the kids did."

"Yes. A good man. But old and not up to coping with Conroy. He killed him."

"Conroy?" Quillen sat up. "Well, good—"

"No. That animal of his did it. With his bare hands. It was terrible." He shuddered, looked at his dead cigar. For a moment he brooded in silence. Then he said, "It was murder. We knew it. We knew who did it. The sheriff came from Tracy and arrested Moriarty and Matt Conroy. We had a trial. I prosecuted, as special attorney for the district. Conroy imported a big lawyer with important eastern connections. Eustace Holman. And ..." the old man pushed the words through a sigh—"they beat us."

Angelarry looked worn out suddenly and old.

"The trial, was it ..."

"Fair?" The lawyer sat back, shrugged. "Last month Eustace Holman was appointed district judge. The sole representative of the judiciary from the Llano Estacado to the western boundary. And to the north, infinitely. Appointed by the military governor, De Puys—the only real law in Case County."

"How could you let this happen? Why wasn't something done?"

"Yes. Why, indeed?" Paul Angelarry's eyes glittered. He leaned forward sharply and barked, "Because we're a conquered people! Captured, beaten, made to comply. *You* can't understand that. What it means to lose. Have it rubbed in your face day after day. Like ripe manure. Conquered!"

He stared at Quillen for a moment; then relaxed, shrugging.

"At any rate, Conroy—through Holman—was and is powerful. He wanted Kewpie. Had no interest in cattle, he said. But he wanted Kewpie. And later events bear him out."

"What events?"

"He runs no cattle of his own on Kewpie grass. I sold all stock under the Q-P brand to a trail-driving rancher from down south. Money's in a New York bank. But that's later. Listen. Conroy had a man named John Bland appointed town marshal. He still is. If you meet him, remember that. He's a Conroy man."

Coy sat up, rubbed at his beard. "Yes. There seems to be quite a few of those around. How did he do it, Paul? Get so powerful in so short a time?"

"Now that's one I've looked at from all angles. Near as I can figure it, he sold someone a bill of goods. Our leading merchants—the town leaders, as it were. He sold them a song of progress and they bought it. Tom Bradford was mayor then. Still is. He's got the biggest store in town, you remember?"

Coy nodded. "The Mercantile Trader's."

"The abolishment of the constitutions," Angelarry went on, "and the consolidation, pushed the pattern out into daylight where men could get a look at a real setup. Sheridan heads the Fifth Military District—that's us. Holman is his judge. Appointed on recommendation of Captain De Puys. Things got a little clearer when they started the manifestoes." He looked at Quillen, eyebrows working. "You see what that means?"

Coy nodded. "Anything goes."

"Anything," Angelarry amended, "that can stand at least perfunctory scrutiny in Santa Fe. And how close do they look when they've got a man on the scene?"

"De Puys." Quillen pocketed his pipe, studied the lawyer gravely. "Is he in it, too? Captain De Puys?"

"Nobody knows. It doesn't seem likely. You see, he's an academy man. Regular army and all that. But you see what happened? All Conroy wanted was Kewpie. From the first. The rest was window dressing."

Quillen dropped his head into his hands. "So Conroy wanted Kewpie. And he got it. Tell me how, Paul. Exactly how. It doesn't matter. I'll get it back. One way or another. But I'd like to know how he did it."

"The Expropriation Law."

"Ex…"

"Expropriation. A fancy way to steal. It means annexing privately owned land for state purposes. Now usually this is done with indemnification. Purchasing, for a fair and equitable price, the land in question. Expropriation without indemnification was long ago legislated against in this country. But they got around that neatly. And legally. Or at least as legally as the rest of it."

Coy shook his head in bewilderment. "I don't understand. How could they just *take* land?"

"Sit still and I'll tell you. I'm to blame. Nobody else. It was not politic to just seize the land. If they did that, we could appeal to the military supervisor. Phil Sheridan, in this district. General Phil, the Dandy. Had they summarily taken land—any land at all—we would have sent a delegation to Santa Fe and something would have been done. So they drafted a local manifesto. Providing for expropriation with indemnification. Now, this was…"

"But you said…"

"Will you listen! Without indemnification, *on the death of the original holder!* You see? What it amounted to was that the state—that is, the law—could exercise a legal option on grant lands originally belonging to the state or territory on the death of the original grantor!"

"That means nobody can inherit…"

The little man sniffed, nodded. "Lands thus designated and selected. Providing the original patent had been a grant."

Angelarry sat back. He closed his eyes and pulled vaguely at his side-whiskers. Coy rubbed his hand slowly back and forth on the leather arm of the chair. It was cool, slick. Finally he raised his eyes, gazed for a long time at a picture on the wall, never seeing it. A muscle flicked at the side of his cheek.

"And Kewpie?" The words were soft.

The old man nodded. He opened his eyes and let his chin drop to the flowered cravat.

"Yes," he said. "Sam Quillen was dead. They killed Anse Prinell. Kewpie came under the law. Your father and Anse held the original grant jointly."

Coy pushed back against the chair, stayed rigid for a long moment, then he said, "Don't blame yourself. I should have been here. You couldn't have done anything."

"Couldn't have done anything? Do you mean that? You're blind then, boy. Your brains have been jellied by the pounding of those guns you nursed against your brothers."

Quillen flushed, felt his eyes squeeze. Even Paul. The lawyer stood up suddenly behind his massive desk.

"Coy, don't you see? From the moment that law became a reality," he said and it came out in his courtroom voice, rising and resounding: "From that moment—Anse Prinell was doomed!" He sat suddenly in the chair.

The pushing silence was loud in the sunny room. A porcelain clock on the mantelpiece sounded like a shod horse crossing a wooden bridge. Quillen sat without moving.

Finally the lawyer spoke again, slowly, all of the fire burned out. "And that's not all. When the law was passed—the manifesto—I thought it would never stick. Said so. People would rise up and De Puys wouldn't dare ratify. And what's more important, refuse to effect seizures with his troop. That's what I told Anse. You see, he knew. Knew that Conroy wanted Kewpie; knew that only so long as he lived could it be held for you kids. He was the only surviving grant holder. I was wrong. Professionally, grievously wrong."

"Then you were wrong. That's all."

"Coy, I've lived with it until—"

"Well, if you don't quit building it up you'll die with it. Now, go on—tell me chapter and verse so I can get to work doing something about it."

Angelarry looked up. Spots of color showed on each wrinkled cheek. "You won't get anywhere. But I'm happy you want to try."

"I don't want to," Coy burst out. "I *have* to. Now, what else?"

The lawyer shrugged, gnawed at a knuckle. "That's it. They got your ranch."

"Where did it begin? Were there any other confiscations?"

"There were. A few. Prime land on Kewpie's perimeter."

Quillen straightened, his eyes took light. "Paul! Maybe that's a point right there. For appeal, I mean. They wanted Kewpie and nothing else."

"Forget about appeal." The lawyer leaned back. "All there is, is Sheridan. And we've been there. And to Washington, by mail. Washington refers to Sheridan. Sheridan refers to local action. De Puys."

Coy slumped in the chair. "The old political circus," he muttered.

"There was a ridiculous proposal for a state railroad. Giving motive to the land grab, you see. An excuse, of course. And a clumsy one. But enough to cover their tracks for Santa Fe. Honest mistakes in judgment cannot be prosecuted. Holman's idea, probably."

"Where is he?"

"Holman? Making the judicial sweep to the south and east. He'll be in town in a week or two. I asked him at the time if a right-of-way wouldn't have served. The railroad thing, you know. He had no answer. The bastard!"

"Who else?"

"Who else, what? Are bastards?"

"I've met a few. No. Who else got—whatever that word was ..."

"Expropriated ?"

"Yes."

"The Forrestor place went first. Before the Q-P. Then, just last week old Homer Willets died. They're trying to serve the oldest boy now. Chub, they call him. He says he won't move."

"I met him. What happened to Alex Forrestor?"

"Killed. Harley Maddux killed him. In a gunfight. An even break, I believe they call it. It was murder. The bill was invoked. That's what I meant by my earlier mention of the boy, Davey Forrestor. You and he have a lot in common."

"You said Maddux?"

"That's what I said, and I'll say it to his bloodless face, though he hole me where I stand. Shot him down at a dance. Said he insulted him. Davey and the older boy, Babe, went after Maddux. They didn't do so good. Both jumped him. Maddux's good with a gun—real good. Babe died. Davey's just getting over a bullet in his upper chest." The old lawyer shook his head, sighed. "He'll try again."

The dry voice stopped. A tinkle of cutlery came from somewhere in the house and clock sound was loud again. A wagon rolled by in the street, one wheel screeching.

Quillen sat motionless. The bad hand, curved rigid, raked furrows in one trouser leg.

"What're you thinking, boy?"

Coy roused. He gazed out the office window and his voice was far away and bleak, sighing up out of the great chest.

"Well, I think I'll kill Harley Maddux. Just to make a start ..."

CHAPTER 6

"KILLING is a harsh cure, son," the lawyer said.

Quillen sat silently and looked out into the summer sunshine.

"Who is it you're mad at, Coy? Remember, you must know who you're fighting before you can fight."

Coy turned his head to the lawyer, the action stiff and deliberate. "There's no mistake—no question," he said and got up slowly. His right hand rubbed the hip where his gun should have been.

"That hand," Angelarry said. "Is it any good at all?"

It was the first mention of the wound; Coy understood the brusqueness and applauded the old man for it. He shook his head. He lifted the hand, wiggled the thumb up and down.

"That's all. Fingers won't move. Can't squeeze at all. No pressure. Just a hook."

The little man was thoughtful for a moment. After a time he said, "Maddux is an extremely competent gunman."

And he left it there.

"What else is there for me to do?"

"A man always does as his heart dictates—finally. I don't believe you stand a chance. Not against Conroy's professionals. With that hand..." He hunched his shoulders in a quick shrug. "But you'll do what you're pressured into. I've seen it before."

"Paul, a man just can't give up. All my life I've believed in the orderly way. The law is a—well, call it a servant of the people. That's the way I've always seen it. The way Sam Quillen taught me. But I'm no child. I can see the deck in this game is stacked and the chips are high. Yet—I've got to play."

"You won't help anyone unless you stay alive."

Quillen smiled. "I go for that."

"Don't talk around it," Angelarry said testily. "What are you going to do and when?"

"The when is easy. Now. The what is something else. There is no legal answer, you're sure of that?"

"None."

"If I personally got it before the land commissioner?"

"No. That's flat and final. There is no land office as you knew it. There are no state offices. We're under martial law, I told you. All law is administered through the military. Here, that's Captain Peter De Puys."

The lawyer spun away. His head bobbed and the white side-whiskers bristled. He turned back to Quillen, forehead wrinkled.

"Listen. There's one thing. A very slim possibility."

"Anything," Coy said, leaning forward. His fingers gripped the desk. "Anything at all ..."

"You might file a petition in restraint of attachment. Give a copy to De Puys and one to Holman. Tell both of them you're taking another in person to General Sheridan in appeal from local action. I don't know what good it would do. If any. De Puys will naturally defend his position. And Holman, his judge. But it's something."

"You have no faith in this?"

"None." He pushed back from the desk. "Not one tasseled little whit!"

Coy nodded slowly, thoughtfully. "Won't do no good," he said. "But it might make them nervous. It might do that."

Paul Angelarry fidgeted behind his oversized desk. He pulled at his whiskers. A bell rang in the street as a boy drove a bunch of milkers past the house. The lawyer rapped his knuckles on the desk.

"The petition. Didn't you hear …"

Quillen shrugged and bent backward from the waist, stretching. Tendons cracked loudly. "We'll see," he said, and moved to the window, walking heavily.

A dusky bird pecked at a mound in the rutted street. The sun was high. "What about Lydia?"

It was a long moment before the lawyer spoke. Coy caught a low-voiced curse before: "Well? What about her?"

"She's still part of Kewpie. Half belongs to her and her mother."

"That young lady forfeited any rights she ever had when she went to Conroy." Rage deepened the old man's voice and Quillen turned to face him. "Her mother, yes," Angelarry said. "The girl, absolutely not!"

"Did you ever think, Paul, that maybe—just maybe—she had a reason for what she did?"

Paul Angelarry drew himself up behind the massive desk. His eyes looked straight at Quillen and there was no compromise in them. "There can be no reason," he said with finality.

Coy turned away. "It's easy to judge. Let's see what happens, what the future brings."

"She has no future. Only a past." The words were soft, without heat.

There was a noise in the hall and the lawyer cursed someone's eternal clumsiness. Sounded like someone falling down the narrow stairs into the front hall.

"Now, what's that?" he asked, as he started out from behind the desk. The door opened and Bud Quillen appeared in the doorway. His face was flushed and sweat-slicked. He wore a pair of almost new gray trousers striped in gold and a soft gray shirt. His brown curls hung over his forehead and he weaved slightly on heeled boots.

"It's me," he said, glaring into the room. "Only me. The dumb brother. I'm leaving."

"Leaving? Why that's silly, boy. Where would you go? Now don't be foolish…"

Bud hitched his weapon belt around on lean hips. He jerked his chin at Coy.

"Him," he said. "He'll be stayin' here. So I'm not. I'll be at the Canadian House, anybody asks."

"Bud—"

"I got nothing to say to you." The boy's voice was thick with alcohol. He looked at Coy. A sick hatred suffused the normally clean-cut features. "Nothing at all."

"Bud," Coy said quietly, "there's no use in this. No sense. I'll go. If you can't stay under the same roof with me, why I'll leave. Not you."

"Now, wait," the lawyer said. "There's no—"

"You don't tell me what to do any more, Coy," Bud said. "Understand? No more. Telling me who I can talk about—threatening me. It's always been like that." Bud's face worked. He leveled a finger at Coy. "But no more. Not a damn bit more. If you wasn't crippled, I'd shoot you down and never miss the ball!"

"Bud!" Coy took a half-step toward the door.

"Leave me alone. Just leave me alone—hear?"

For a moment Bud regretted the action he was taking. Coy saw it. The thought washed across his open face like a cloud shadow on a sunny hill. Then he glanced at Quillen's hand, swung away.

Coy said, "What about our ranch, Bud?"

The kid paused, not turning. "Well, what about it? It's gone, ain't it? You gonna get it back? Talk 'em out of it, maybe? You always was quite a talker, Coy."

"I'm going to try. Talking or—or otherwise."

"Try then," Bud said, and left.

Angelarry and Coy stood for a long moment; neither spoke. The outside door slammed. Quillen went to the window, an obscure urge pushing him—like the desire to run alongside a train for a last look at a friend.

"You'd like to wash up. Shave, I guess," the little lawyer said.

"Yes," Coy said.

Through the window he watched his brother's high-shouldered, slender figure swaggering in the street, arms full of personal gear. In his hand he carried a slim, curved Confederate saber in a fancy scabbard. The boy cavalryman. Captain Quillen of the Second Texas. A long, gold tassel hung from the saber's hilt, swinging with the young man's progress. Coy turned from the window.

The noon sun hung high in hard blue that seemed to have no dimension. Off in the west a heavy pall of dust hovered over the plain. Coy had noted it earlier when he rode out to recover his saddle and warbags. Now, standing in the street before the Drover's Rest, he shaded his eyes and squinted in that direction, trying to position the haze. Dust it was. A yellow layer separating the vivid blue of the sky and the plain's greenish summer-brown.

"Cattle on Kewpie," he muttered. "If I didn't know better, I'd say that..."

Paul had told him of the disposition of Kewpie cattle. He'd told him also that Conroy ran no cattle of his own on the Kewpie range.

"Hey! Your name Quillen?"

Coy heard the shout but he didn't turn right away. His hand fumbled with the reins, pulled his horse up beside him.

"You hear me, buster?"

Quillen turned then. Slowly, face composed. It had been a heavy voice and the man standing on the board sidewalk gazing truculently at him was all of that. He was a tall man, big in the shoulders, with a paunch that pushed aside soiled wings of a leather vest. A tarnished star drooped on the vest.

John Bland, Quillen thought, remembering Angelarry's story about old Charlie Morris. Bland was a bearded man, puffy-eyed and thick-lipped, wearing a serviceable-looking frontier model Colt low on his right thigh. The weapon belt ran under the man's protruding stomach, emphasizing the size of it. Little red eyes peered at Quillen from nests of puffy white.

"You fixin' to answer my question?"

"Why?" Quillen asked quietly. He moved toward the man, pulling the horse along behind.

"Why?" The heavy man stepped to the street, hand hanging stiffly by his holster. "Well, now, I reckon because, by God, I asked you."

Quillen looked down at his bare hip. He had no weapon save the Henry rifle sticking in his saddle scabbard.

"That so?"

He turned back to the hitch-pole, tied the horse with a flip of the rein. He started across the street to the Drover's Rest. Bland interposed his bulk, stopped Quillen in the dust of the street. They stood chest to chest.

"I got an idea," the marshal said, blaring out the words, "you and me ain't gonna get along at all. Not at all. When I ask you a question"—he tapped the tarnished star with a thumb—"you answer it. That clear?"

Along the street all activity stopped. Tom Bradford, florid moon of a face grinning with pleasure, leaned in the doorway of the Mercantile, his expression almost shouting how glad he was to see a Quillen get comeuppance. Idlers appeared and windows were suddenly filled with curious eyes. Coy was aware that the group on the porch of the Drover's Rest had risen. Some of them drifted into the street.

Quillen looked into the marshal's red eyes with a flat stare. He said nothing.

"You hear me, renegade?" The thrusting belly touched Coy. "When I speak, Quillen, damn you, jump!" the fat man stormed.

"You knew my name, then?" Coy questioned quietly.

"You damned right," Bland wheezed. "And your history. Turncoat! What's this about starting trouble in Mr. Conroy's place last night?"

"Last night?"

"You heard me!"

"Why didn't you ask me last night?"

Bland stared. Then he said, "What you tryin' to say, Quillen?"

"I'm saying you're a puppet and a fat slob of a puppet, at that. I'm saying if you had a charge against me it should have been last night, not today after you talked with Matt Conroy."

"Just a minute—"

"One more thing I'm saying…" Quillen leaned forward slightly. His eyes, cold and dark, bored into the marshal's. "Get your blubber-gut out of my way. You're standing where I aim to walk."

Bland sputtered. Finally his lips made words. "Why, you scum!"

The marshal twisted, clawing for his long-barreled pistol. Quillen watched the fat man's hand fumble with the gun butt. He didn't move. But he was ready without appearing to be. Weight balanced over his feet, legs solidly planted. He waited. It was a faculty he'd employed to good advantage in countless bar and camp brawls and now he was ready.

"He ain't got no gun, Marshal!" a man shouted.

Bland's hand dragged at his Colt. He said, "I'll blow your—"

And Quillen struck. As the fat man's gun cleared leather, Coy reached out and grasped it tightly and whipped the bad hand around in a vicious backhand clout. Bland, turned by the force of the blow, almost fell and his pistol came away in Coy's hand. He stepped in and lifted his knee, slamming it into the marshal's bulging stomach. Breath whistled and the man bent forward in agony, bringing his head low. Quillen moved back, measured coolly and swung his left hand, gun and all.

It had taken only a watch tick. The watchers had hardly drawn a breath at the first blow when the fight was over. The man fell, bleeding badly, and Coy looked up, instantly wary. The gun was heavy in his hand. He flipped it and caught it in shooting position in his left hand. The blue muzzle weaved and Quillen waited. Nobody said a word.

Then the group on the porch broke into loud jeers at the spectacle of the lawman wallowing in the dust, dripping blood.

"Look at ol' puss-gut," one shouted. "Lookin' for clues."

A laugh went up. Other sallies followed. Conroy's man, Moriarty, stood in the doorway of the Drover's Rest, watching without expression. He had no gun. None that Quillen could see. He turned back inside the saloon as Coy's eyes met his.

Davy Forrestor dropped off the walk behind Coy. Quillen saw the movement out of the corner of his eye. The youngster had circled during the fight, coming up from the plain's side. Quillen had no idea why.

"This any of your put-in?" he asked the slim puncher.

The young man shook his head, stood spraddle-legged and nodded slowly at the figure in the dust. An expression of satisfaction flitted over his tanned face, gone in an instant. He rocked slightly, lean body inclined back from the hips, thumbs hooked in a shelled gunbelt.

"You're learnin', Yankee," he said. "Damned if you ain't learnin'."

Coy looked at him, started to speak. Forrestor's eyes stayed on the marshal. Coy grunted instead, walked to. the dazed officer. Bland stirred and sat up. His face dripped blood and an angry welt ran from forehead to chin; some of the ratty beard had been scraped away.

"Assault," he said weakly, cringing away from Quillen. "You're under arrest. You can't—"

Coy laughed, stuffing the captured pistol into his waistband. "Marshal, next time you see me, you arrest me. Right now, I'm busy. And when you do it, don't forget to take off your hat."

He flipped the man's black felt to the ground, stepped on it, walking away toward the saloon.

There was a stir in the silent mob and Chub Willets pushed to the front of the group. He glared as Coy mounted the steps. A splotch of purple darkened the right side of his face. Quillen tightened his grip on the gun butt.

Chub spoke loudly, with clear precision: "You are a Yankee-lovin' sonofabitch!" he said. "Now let's see you take *my* hat off."

He crouched expectantly, hand curling around a walnut gun butt. As he did, Quillen jerked and leveled the pistol he'd taken from Bland, cocking it with the side of his bad hand. The muzzle centered Willets.

"Don't!" he warned.

Chub stopped, gun half drawn. His mouth dropped open. Coy wondered fleetingly what the man would say if he knew that Quillen couldn't hit anything left-handed. Even at this range he wouldn't bet on his accuracy. He had never fired a gun from the wrong side.

But nobody moved at all. Coy smiled thinly and indicated the fat man with the bleeding face, standing uncertainly in the street.

"Not interested in your hat, Chub. Just his."

He pushed the gun back into his waistband and stepped through the swinging doors into the dead quiet Drover's Rest.

CHAPTER 7

Sergeant Eldred O'Bain cocked a grizzled eyebrow at his drinking companion and wrapped a huge fist around a whisky glass.

"Mr. Quillen," he said, brass cavalry tones ringing in the room, "here's to more polite marshals."

He hoisted and drank and Quillen smiled. The Drover's Rest had been quite well-populated when he stalked in after his brush with the marshal a half hour before. The cavalry sergeant, whom Quillen recognized as the same steady noncom who had backed Captain De Puys so effectively, had insisted on buying him a drink. He bought one in return. Several drinks and many battle stories later, they were well on the way to becoming fast friends. Wartime reminiscence comes easy. Both had fought on the same fields.

"Bartender," Quillen called. "Do it again here."

He put his back to the bar and hooked elbows on the rail. The pistol butt showed black against his white shirt. The marshal had not followed him into the saloon. It was better that he hadn't . . . .

Quillen's eyes roved the room. It was crowded. Very crowded for an afternoon. There seemed to be a repressed sort of gaiety and expectation evident. Coy wondered why. Troops of flashily-dressed girls added their shrillness to the mixed sound. It was an unhealthy noise, much of it forced. Quillen watched the gilded spokes of the Big Six wheel clack round, flashing; faro dealers called the box for an already brisk play.

O'Bain rattled on and Quillen nodded and grunted in the right places. His eyes continued to play about the large room. He had not seen Conroy. Moriarty stood, hulking and primordial, at the other end of the bar. Drank nothing, did nothing; just stood, pig eyes gleaming. Coy turned back to his companion.

"O'Bain," he interrupted, "what do you think of De Puys?"

A quick look. "Ah, now. Should you be askin' me that, Sergeant?"

"I'm not questioning your loyalty. But—well, you know what happened to me. To my ranch."

O'Bain's firm, ruddy face creased with sympathy. "I do," he said. He slugged down his whisky. "Aye, I do, indeed."

"And do you know that De Puys is the reason for it? I don't say that he's mixed in it. I don't believe that. But he's being led by unscrupulous people. Misplacing his trust, taking bad advice maybe."

The big Irishman scowled at his empty glass. He pushed back his forage cap from the mop of red-gray hair.

"Ah, you sure make it hard on a man, Coy Quillen. Would you be changin' the subject? For a favor?"

The barman poured two drinks in answer to a hand summons. He glanced at the two big men, not bothering to conceal his enmity. He poured sloppily and the liquor spilled. O'Bain stiffened and would have spoken. Quillen touched his arm. He nodded toward the door where two shotgun guards sat, flanking the entrance. Then his eyes flicked upward to the rear balcony. A young cowboy prowled ceaselessly, dressed ordinarily except for belted pistols and a rifle carried in the crook of one arm. Quillen shook his head warningly at O'Bain.

"That's what they want," he said. "It's a fort, this place."

"And it had better be," the sergeant offered. "One day, Quillen—mark me, lad—these men will take this place apart. Plank by plank, whore by pimp!"

"What men?"

"What men? Why, Forrestor and his bully-lads. Why do you suppose they hang about outside? Because they like the atmosphere? Pah! They're warmin' their rightful hatred by wallowin' in their own disgrace. It's primin' themselves, they are."

Quillen scowled at his drink. "Law of the gun. Always the goddam gun!"

O'Bain faced him seriously, his great green eyes clear as a Texas morning. "Was there ever any other kind?" he asked softly.

Coy looked at the cavalryman. He had no answer. Once he could have answered. Not now. Especially not now.

"About the men," he said. "Forrestor—the rest. You may be right. I wondered about that."

"Oh, I'm right, right enough. You take that Forrestor. Officially the Army can't have him takin' the law into his own hands. Him and his friends. The captain ordered him watched for trouble. But it'll do no good, lad. None at all." The sergeant glanced at Quillen. "Officially, that is. But a man's sympathies are his own."

"Yes," Quillen said. He picked up his drink.

"About the captain," O'Bain offered, breaking in on Coy's thoughts. "I've known him but shortly. But he commands." He searched Quillen's eyes. "You understand?"

"Of course." And he did. He sipped his whisky. "O'Bain, do you think the law is a just one that takes a man's land for a thief's profit?"

"The questions you ask, lad. What I think is not important. It's what I'm ordered to do that counts. As you well know, being the Army man you are. I've fought with the Fifth Pennsylvania. And I've seen your brave black cross flyin' in many's the smoke. Why, at Malvern Hill when—" he stopped suddenly. "But never mind the war. The faster it's forgot, the better."

"For me," Coy agreed.

"Aye, and for all of us. What I was gettin' to was this, now—when Charlie Griffin bawled an order, you didn't think about how you felt about it. Did you now?"

"I understand, O'Bain." He pounded his palm on the pistol butt. "But how could it happen? How could men stand by and let things get so sour that honest soldiers are forced to do the filthy work of a Bowery thief!"

A silence settled over the room. It was unnatural and sudden. O'Bain nodded at Quillen's statement and reached for his drink, unaware of any change. But Quillen's back prickled. He knew something had happened; he didn't know what. He eased his hand to the pistol butt. He pivoted, ready for whatever was to come. Conroy had finally arrived.

"Being complimentary again, Quillen? A failing you'd do well to correct."

Matt Conroy's voice knifed the smoky atmosphere in the big, now silent room. He stood on the balcony, flanked by two men, gazing at the room below. One dainty boot tapped. Otherwise his calm superiority was unmarred. The brown eyes came back to Quillen and O'Bain and he spoke again through the haze separating them.

"But then, I see you've found your own level."

O'Bain, who had stiffened at the first words, now turned, hands hanging loose at his sides. Quillen put out a hand, stopped him. His eyes were riveted on the three men descending the balcony stairs. Conroy, Harley Maddux—the pale-haired killer.

And Bud Quillen.

Three abreast, the gently smiling Conroy slightly ahead of the others, they crossed the motionless room. Coy ripped out a low curse, stifled it. But he didn't move. He stood, and hoped his rock face did not pick this moment to betray him.

The trio halted a few feet from the two men at the bar. Customers on both sides began easing away. The few troopers scattered throughout the room straightened alertly, hitching at their weapons. They looked to O'Bain. The Irishman's face was twisted with a contempt he was too honest to hide.

Conroy didn't bother to look at the soldier. He pushed aside his coat and shoved tiny hands into the pockets of his tailored, cream-colored trousers.

"Well, Quillen. I hear you're re-educating marshals now. Got started quickly. Something about etiquette, wasn't it?" He smiled. But the brown eyes remained cold.

Coy ignored Conroy. He looked at his brother. Bud's face was sullen and loose. He had been drinking. He still wore gray and a new revolver hung at his right hip. He refused to meet his brother's eyes. Maddux, standing hip-shot at Conroy's right hand, laughed, seeing the byplay. The laugh was soft and insulting. Coy drew himself up, balanced. His hand gripped the gun.

O'Bain heaved his bulk forward a step, slid in front of Coy. "Conroy," he said loudly. "You'll be noticin' I have on me hip a non-regulation Colt forty-four." He paused. "And two good hands on me arms."

He stopped. His lips matched Conroy's smile. There was at once no sound at all. Even the gamblers grew still. Then Maddux growled and dipped; Conroy grabbed his sleeve, stopping him.

"Let him go, Conroy," O'Bain rumbled, eyes on Maddux. "Turn the bully-boy loose. I'd be happy to have him wearin' my mark."

"Easy, easy," Conroy said. He took out a slim cigar, fingered it. "I don't think you'd better come in here, Quillen. Things happen where you are. You'd oblige me by staying out."

Coy looked at his brother, tried to catch his eye. But his words were directed to Conroy.

"I came for the gun you took from me the other night," he said. "If you'll give it to me, I'll leave."

"Of course," Conroy said. He nodded. The bartender reached under the bar and came up with Quillen's gunbelt and the Navy Colt. It thumped on the bar. Coy didn't turn.

"But," Conroy went on, "I believe you have a pistol there which belongs to one of my men. Could I have it?"

"I just wanted to hear you say that, Conroy."

"All right. I've said it. He's my man and that's his gun. I'm pretty sure he'll have use for it—and soon."

Coy pulled the pistol from his waistband. He twirled it on a thick finger, dropped it to the floor. Matt Conroy stuck the cigar between his teeth. The smile framed it. He took out a match, his eyes never leaving Coy.

"You're determined, big fella. I can see that. I told you not to buck me. All you can do is make it hard on yourself. You won't listen. All right. I won't tell you again. As for you, Sergeant..." He looked at O'Bain, shook his head chidingly.

"Oh, now wait," the Irishman said, stepping forward. "Let's be gettin' something straight here." The sergeant's square jaw jutted and anger showed in the set of his body. "You'll not be puttin' your footmarks on O'Bain. Not now—or later. If you've a mind for trouble, turn it loose. For I'm not your man. You'll steal no land from me!"

A murmur ran through the room. The half dozen or so troopers sidled for position, fondling their weapons. If O'Bain fell, lead would fly in earnest. Maddux looked up sharply and seemed to sniff the air. The undercurrent grew, an ugly sound.

"All I need is the word, Matt," Maddux said, eyes on O'Bain. His hand curled near the open-faced holster on his hip.

Quillen stepped out from behind the cavalryman, weaponless, his Colt behind him on the bar.

"Wait!" Conroy called sharply.

Maddux stopped; O'Bain held the same ready position. No one moved in the room. Conroy clamped down on the thin cigar. The easy smile was gone.

"I steal land from no one, O'Bain," he said, clear tones overriding the beginning crowd murmur. "I'm a businessman. That's all. And I want no fight in my place of business. So let's have a drink and forget this talk of trouble." He looked around slowly; there was now no sound, no movement. "You too, big fella.

Everybody have one. Bartender! Drinks for everyone—on Matt Conroy."

He struck a match, said to Maddux, "Put that thing away." The match climbed to the cigar tip, lit it, flame steady.

There was a rush for the bar and the hot moment passed. Quillen got his gunbelt off the bar and around his hips. He fumbled with the bad hand. The buckle took time. When it was done he took the Navy Colt out of the leather and stuck it into his belt in front. Then he looked to his brother.

"Bud," he said quietly, "have you thought about what you're doing?"

Bud glanced at Conroy quickly, then at Coy. He wet his lips with flicking tongue. "I know," he said, and left it there.

"Just be sure, Bud. And remember where we stand. Each of us."

"Sure, Coy," he said, leaning forward. "I'll remember. Like you did in the war—against my own!"

Coy pushed away from the bar. His face felt lumpy and his back was wet. He faced his brother. "Why, Bud?"

Bud Quillen hooked his thumbs in side pockets. To his credit, he managed a smile. Lips pulled away from set teeth, he spoke quietly, the words carrying in the velvet silence.

"I'll tell you why, too, brother. Because ol' Bud ain't gonna be on the losin' side no more."

He lifted his head, raised his voice.

"A loser don't ever get through paying," he said.

CHAPTER 8

THE PARLOR was painfully neat, stuffed with an assortment of ancient furniture. One small window admitted all of the light the room could stand. Mrs. Prinell sat in a high-backed chair and worked automatically at a large piece of embroidery. She was a tall woman, large-boned and capable appearing, with a smooth bun of white hair and clear, widely-spaced gray eyes. She had been a beautiful woman, accomplished and well-bred, and she hadn't let the hard life of the plains drain her to sallow listlessness.

Coy sat on the edge of a hard chair, acutely conscious of the woman. Lydia's mother. He twirled the black hat between his fingers. His eyes followed the swiftly-moving hands on the embroidery frame.

"Well, Coy," the woman's rich tones brought his head up. She looked at him, smiled sadly. "What are you going to do?"

Someday he'd find an answer to that one. Everyone seemed to ask that question when they talked to him. Even O'Bain.

They had left the Drover's Rest after the incident with Bud and Conroy, both shaken by the experience. The sergeant had held his anger and intended to dissipate it in a drinking bout. Coy refused an invitation to go with him, thinking of the duty call to be made on Mrs. Prinell.

They stood for a moment in the square before parting. Thunder grew from the direction of Kewpie. Coy nudged O'Bain.

"What's that?"

The cavalryman needed only a brief glance. He turned to Quillen and the set of his mouth was grim.

"What is that indeed," he said.

The roar grew as they waited and soon a rushing charge of whooping horsemen slammed into Two Trees, shaking windows and sending teams into panic. The riders poured past the square, rustling the trees with their wind; lean men, dirty and bearded and trail-worn, mounted on tough range ponies. They yipped and swung hats. One or two fired pistols into the air. Quillen understood now why there'd been so many girls in the Drover's Rest. Conroy's coffers would tinkle this night.

O'Bain put his lips next to Coy's ear.

"Trail herd," he said. "They must have quite a bunch. I counted twenty-two riders."

"Twenty-two! Where could they bed a herd that size?"

The sergeant turned away. He straightened his forage cap on the shock of red-gray hair and looked back at Quillen from under the short peak.

"Kewpie," he said. He faced his friend, green eyes watchful and caring. "What are you going to do, Mr. Quillen?"

Mr. Quillen wished he knew.

He spun the hat and looked at the white-haired lady in the light of the Morlys' parlor. He shook his head.

"Well, what is there to do, Aunt May?"

The woman smiled, a singularly lovely and transforming smile, and suddenly you knew where her daughter had caught her dark spark of beauty.

"That's up to you," the woman said. "You're a man. And your father's son. You'll do what you have to."

"What if—I mean it's not right that I endanger your property by my actions. Kewpie is all you have. Me—well, it makes no difference about me. Aunt May—they call me a renegade."

"And does that make it so?"

"No. But it means I'll get no help, no sympathy."

Taut cloth vibrated under flying fingers. "Whatever you do—it's for all of us. The responsibility is yours."

"Mine?"

"Of course. We've been over this, Coy. The ranch is ours. No piece of paper can change that. Your father and my husband built it. No paper can cover Kewpie. It's too big." She looked up from her work. "And it's not only us, Coy. Everyone has suffered. They're our people—they look to us."

"No! They're not our people. What did—"

"They are!" the woman said, iron in her rich voice. "Kewpie has always been the giant. There's been no change. Because your father and—and Anse, are gone, is no excuse for giving up. We must not give up. We must not be false to our charge."

"I'll fight no fight but my own. Did they hang Anse Prinell's killer? Did they save your ranch?"

He. rose abruptly, suddenly confined and restricted and needing room. He crushed the hat under his arm and stalked to the window.

"Coy," Mrs. Prinell said softly. "Come here and sit down." She laid aside her work. "No, Coy, they did none of those things. And I didn't expect them to. For I knew they could not. Don't you see? No man among them is strong enough to weld a common effort. And that's why the responsibility is Kewpie's." She nodded at him, eyes brimming suddenly. "Yours, Coy. You *are* Kewpie now."

Quillen looked out the window, seeing the sky and the far purple horizon. After a time he said, "What about Bud?"

"That's something I can't answer, Coy," the woman said softly. "He was here all along. And yet ..."

Coy nodded. He sought the woman's eyes. His bad hand, the fingers half-clenched and rigid, came up slowly between them.

"And this? Is there no allowance for being without tools?"

She took the hand in her own cool ones and held it firmly. But she didn't look at it. She looked instead at his face and he felt that it must appear hard and ugly. Her lips quirked.

"It doesn't matter."

"Doesn't matter? Conroy has professional gunmen. Maddux and Bland. A bad kid named Lupo. And another, Tal Everest. Maybe more O'Bain didn't know about. How can I fight such men with one hand?"

"I don't say you'll fight, Coy. Only that you will do what has to be done."

She straightened in the chair and pushed his hand away from her.

"Tools," she said. "Don't talk to me of tools. You do what you must and you use what you have. That's the way it is."

Lydia's mother watched him and her erect shoulders squared even more. Quillen looked at her and saw a willowy girl in a shadowed room, lamplight streaming on classic features etched with anguish.

"You know about Lydia," he said.

The white bun dipped in a short nod. The woman's smooth cheeks showed tear streaks in the weak light.

"Of course," she whispered. "How could I not know? She's my daughter."

"But how—I mean, you knew she was living with Conroy. You knew all the time." Quillen rose with the words, towered over her. "You let her do it?"

"Sit down!" The words slapped at him. Mrs. Prinell's eyes were ice, her mouth a grim line. "Sit down, I say!"

And he sat.

"Listen. When Anse was killed I wanted to go after Conroy with a pistol. Because I knew that he was to blame no matter who fired the shot. Lydia stopped me. We had no man. And my daughter vowed herself to vengeance. I've never seen her like that. Plotting to meet the man, entice him. And then kill him."

Mrs. Prinell bowed her head for a moment, then went on. "Yes. I knew my daughter went to Conroy. And I knew why. I was hurt, of course—and proud. Proud, do you hear? Can you

understand what strength it must take to face the fiercest humiliation a woman can suffer? Only to fight—to strike back." The
woman slumped in the chair, spent suddenly.

"Your poor, wounded hand, you say. Tools! My God ..."

Coy stared. He leaned toward the silently weeping woman.
"You knew," he said, wonderingly.

"Yes, I knew." She sat up and brushed at her white crown of
hair. "And there's this thought on my mind. If Lydia had been a
boy, there'd be no need for you, Coy Quillen."

"Where is she?" Coy asked, intent and sure for the first time
since his homecoming. "Where's Lydia?"

The woman, pridefully erect and staring at a life long gone,
made no answer. She focused on Quillen.

"And you," she said. "She'd be at your side, if you'd let her. She
loved you always. Never any other. That's the way it was intended,
Lydia and Coy. If there's a change it won't be of her making. At
your side. And that's the way it should be." She looked away. "If
she had been a boy ..."

The silence was unbroken. No outside sounds penetrated.
Quillen's mind raced with thoughts and uncalled memories. It
was hard for him to believe there was, or could be, anything but
this room, this indomitable woman, this hurting man.

A new voice cut through the quiet.

"And I will anyway, Coy," Lydia said from the doorway. "Ride
with you. If you'll let me."

Quillen turned toward the girl standing in the doorway. Her
chin was steady and lifted.

"But I'm afraid I'll never be a boy ..."

Coy lifted his arms and she rushed to them. He held her
tight, closing his eyes against the pleasure of the moment. In her
hair he murmured, "Lydia, Lydia ..."

She molded to him, standing in the dowdy parlor, and her
mouth was cushioned fire melting his rigid lips. He kissed her
again and again.

"Oh, Coy," she whispered. "I thought you'd never come!"

"You knew I'd be back," Coy said. "The night I left—you remember that night?"

Lydia hid her face in his chest. Her head bobbed. Pink crept up in the smooth cheeks. Quillen stroked her firm back, pulling her to him.

"That night lasted me a long time," he said. "Remembering it. Long nights in the lines. Even longer ones in the hospital. You were all I thought about."

The girl moved away slightly. Then she reached out both hands, framed his face with them tenderly. For a long while neither moved. Then she moved her lips slowly up to his.

"Wait," she said, breaking away. "Coy, wait. I must tell you. About Conroy. What happened with him—"

"Don't, Lyd!"

"Yes," she said, pulling away. "Just this once. Then no more, ever."

She smoothed her dress automatically and glanced around. Mrs. Prinell had left the room. The ancient parlor was dim, foreign. Lydia moved from him and took the chair her mother had vacated.

"No," she said. "Stay away, darling. Please. Let me tell it—all the way through.

"I waited, Coy," she began. "Oh, so long. Long years. The war was over and I wanted you home. Then as time went on, I began to despair. But I waited anyway. There was no one else for me—could never be. Then"—her eyes narrowed—"they killed my father. And I lost faith, Coy. I wrote a long letter to you—bitter and wild and full of the horror I was living. A terrible letter."

"I didn't get it."

"I'm glad. It was nasty. The ranch was threatened and Dad was dead—and I had no man. I thought the world had ended."

"Lydia, I'm ashamed. I should have come home. But I was afraid. I re-enlisted for two years until things became more settled. My place was here. I was wrong to stay away."

"Yes, Coy, you should have been here. Because when I saw Bud would do nothing but make noises and drink whisky, I decided that finding my father's killer was up to me."

She twisted her hands together, raised her eyes. Quillen longed to reach out to her. But some strange wisdom, a silent warning, told him not to. This was a moment she had to get through alone.

"There was nothing to do but try," she said. "I didn't admit there was much of a chance. But I was certain if I could get close enough to Conroy I'd find out who killed my father." Her eyes glowed in the shadow. "And I did. When you came, I was ready. Oh, I was dramatizing it maybe, building it up. But I had myself convinced I didn't count for anything—that the only important thing was to get even."

Lydia bent her head into cupped hands for a moment. She went on without looking up, tones muffled.

"You came home. Everything changed. I wanted desperately to turn back the clock. Conroy was nothing to me. He had my body. But my heart ..."

Quillen groaned.

"Wait!" she cried. "Let me finish. When I left you in that room last night, I had already left Conroy. You were back. That was enough for me. Nothing else was important. Not even what I'd found out—that Dad's killer was Harley Maddux."

Her eyes came up. The name drifted between them as if she had written it in smoke, left it hanging. Coy sat back and his bad hand crept to the gun at his side.

"Yes, Coy, Harley Maddux! Father was killed at extreme range by a very small-bore ball. A special rifle. Yesterday, at the ranch, I found the gun. And it belonged to Maddux. An English saddle rifle. A gift from Conroy. I asked and he told me."

"Maddux," Quillen said. His face set, stiffened. "What did you do?"

"I wanted to kill him. But I was afraid. Not physically, but afraid I would miss and never get another try. I wanted to be very sure. So I waited for a good chance, a sure chance. And when we got back to town, you were here." She peered deeply into his eyes. "I knew it was no longer up to me. So I left Conroy. When he told you I was his woman, it was a lie. I had left him. You wouldn't listen when I tried to tell you last night. Now perhaps you won't hate me so much."

Quillen stood, looked down at her. He pulled her head hard against his body, pressing.

"Hate you?" he said. "I've never loved anyone else. It's myself I hate. But that's no matter. Not now."

A queer, cold smile crossed his lips. Lydia grasped the bad hand, ran long fingers gently over the massed scar tissue.

"Your hand—it's pretty bad, isn't it? Will you tell me how it happened?"

He pulled her upright and held her close. He shook his head.

"Someday," he said. "But it doesn't matter."

CHAPTER 9

I T WAS quite an encampment. Everything neat and very military. A shake fence ran along the road for a short distance in both directions from a painted gate. The sun, rapidly sliding westward, highlighted a faded flag fluttering at the top of a peeled pine. Two wooden buildings faced the road immediately behind the fence. Behind them, stretching out into the plain, two precise rows of high-sided cantonment tents formed a company street. Farther back and to the east a vast picket line moved with activity.

Quillen sat his horse at the gate and looked the camp over with a soldier's appreciation. He knew how much a military installation reflected the ability and character of its commander. Cavalrymen moved about in disciplined disorder. Coy realized it was almost time for the retreat ceremony.

At the porch of the headquarters building he pulled up. A young trooper stepped forward to hold the mount, his eyes clinging for a moment to the faded stripe on Quillen's trousers. Coy swung to the ground.

"Captain De Puys here?" he asked the youth.

The kid nodded, pointed. "Through that door," he said. "Better hurry. Retreat in ten minutes."

Coy thanked him and clumped inside. He tugged the hat on tightly and fiddled with his gun rig. A heavy-browed sergeant looked up from a wide desk.

"Yes?"

"Captain De Puys. Would you tell him Coy Quillen wants to see him?"

"Quillen?" the noncom laid down his pen and rose. "Right away," he said, and disappeared through a door behind his desk.

Racks of rifles filled the walls of the room. Henrys, Quillen noted. He knew they hadn't been made general issue yet. The racks of new equipment testified to this captain's efficiency or connections—maybe both.

"Mr. Quillen," the sergeant said from the door. "The captain will see you now."

De Puys's office was different. A leather couch and two fat chairs clustered around a small clay fireplace. The walls were hung with pennons and military photographs. On a sideboard a silver cup proclaimed the prowess of Peter De Puys as a pistol shot.

"Well, Mr. Quillen." The captain's voice had a squeak when used conversationally. "I thought you'd be here today. But I looked for you earlier. Sit down. Make yourself comfortable."

"Thanks," Coy said. He sat on a stiff-backed chair near the cluttered desk. "I'll get right to it."

"Fine. What can I do for you? Let me say that I'm happy to see you in spite of the circumstances. Anyone with the moral courage to fight for what he believes, is my friend. This brawling young country needs men with that sort of moral fiber."

"Well, that's big of you." Quillen leaned forward. He didn't like this man. Not at all; and there was no reason he could put a finger on.

"Look here, De Puys. There's no sense in talking all around it. I want to know how legal the attachment of Kewpie is. And I want to know why you ratified it."

The captain stiffened, the smile becoming guarded. "Well, now, Quillen, I'm not required to justify my actions to you. Or to anyone. I doubt very much if I'll tell you *why* I do anything."

"No," Coy said softly. "But you are required to keep order in this district. And I'm in a disorderly mood."

The curve slid from De Puys's lips. He scowled so the mustaches rose at opposite angles.

"Quillen," he said heavily, "I don't think we're going to get along at all."

"That's fine. I'm not running for anything. Or from anything either. It's time someone made a move around here. And it might be me. I don't like that, but it might be there's no other way. You better think about it."

"Indeed?" The officer shifted his weight in the leather chair. "What makes you think I'll listen to your trouble-making? We've been getting on well in this section. General Sheridan is quite pleased with me. Unrest at a minimum, town growing. Now you come along fancying yourself a messiah. I'm not sure I like that."

Quillen stared. The captain drummed on the desk with his fingers and looked blandly at his visitor.

"De Puys, are you blind?" Quillen burst out. "Or only a damn fool? How can you say something like 'getting on well' without choking?"

"Now, see here..."

"No! You see here." Quillen moved forward on the chair. "Murders and land-grabbing. You call that getting on well? Anse Prinell, and Babe Forrestor and his father. How many more? Land stolen, water rights ignored, trail herds laying waste to the grass, and murder in the streets. Unrest at a minimum, is it!"

Quillen slammed out of the chair, stalked to the wall and back. The captain pulled at his mustaches. Coy pinned him with a pointed finger.

"If it is," he said, "I'll take Gettysburg, any time."

"Please, please," the officer said. "These matters are jurisdictional. This is local reprisal action. I can't interfere unless the marshal or some other vested local authority requests it. I know what you feel, man. And as a veteran, you have my sympathy. But I'm actually without power to act. My activities must be confined to the military milieu." De Puys rose and walked to the window. "You know that, Quillen."

"And the manifestoes? How about those?"

The officer considered that. The back of his neck grew slowly red. He clasped hands behind his wide back and stared into the company street. A mounted troop racketed by the window, sabers jangling. He turned.

"All right," he said. "I'm going to tell you. I don't approve the local happenings. Not at all. But since you brought up the ratification …" He returned to the desk, perched on a corner. "Holman drafted the manifesto. He's the legal authority in this district. I know nothing of civil law. I was told—and I checked, Quillen— that a state railroad was advisable. To this purpose a law had to be drawn affording the government legal right to appropriate private land. What happened to the plan, I don't know."

"De Puys, have you ever heard of easement? In law? Or the right of eminent domain?"

"Yes. And I agree a right-of-way was all that should have been necessary. If a railroad really was planned. But—"

"Railroad!" Coy twisted angrily and paced the room, unable to remain still. "That's the goddamndest excuse for grand larceny I've ever heard! A railroad from where? Connecting what?" He stopped before De Puys, glaring at the man. "There's no stick of tie or metal rail in five hundred miles. A thousand! And you know it!"

"I know," the fat officer admitted. He ran nervous fingers over the curving mustaches. "But the reason was unimportant. The manifesto was drafted and submitted. I signed it into law as the proxy of General Sheridan. I did so after careful consideration. Now you can't get around that. Right or wrong, there it is."

Coy swore.

"Yes. You maybe feel different. But consider my position. My district judge recommended and wrote out a law. I could see no reason not to ratify. No one came forward against the bill.

It wasn't the first one. Manifestoes had been used with great success. There has to be some method of law, Quillen. Perhaps I erred in trusting Holman. But I did what I thought was right. And I'm still not sure it was the wrong thing."

"Not sure? After what's happened?"

"All right," De Puys said, leaning forward, his eyes challenging. "What has happened? That you—or anybody—can prove?"

Quillen stood before him, controlling himself with an effort.

"First," he said, "expropriation. On condition that original grantor dies. Is this the way to get railroad land?"

"Now, wait—"

"Railroads run in a line. Whatever you say, people don't conveniently die in a straight line! Not without help, they don't."

"No accusations now. Without proof—"

"Second," Coy said, overriding him, "two men who fit the conditions of this bill die violently. And conveniently. Third—and damn you, get away from this!—the same man winds up with all the land!"

Outside a bugle chattered. De Puys slid off the desk. He mopped his florid face with a neckerchief and turned to face Quillen.

"You're not suggesting a connection?" His eyes hardened. He was suddenly no longer a fat man in a blue uniform, but an officer of the United States Army. An angry one. "Do you believe the Army would be a party to such a thing?" He thrust his face close to Quillen's. "Do you?"

Coy licked his lips. He wanted to lash out, to smash something. But he didn't move. For a tense moment he and De Puys matched glances. Then Quillen relaxed.

"No, Captain," he said, "I don't. I never have. But something is wrong as hell around here. Conroy is bedding trail herds on Kewpie. That's why he wanted it. It's big and it has water. The punchers spend their money in his saloons. Or he robs them at his tables. He charges for the grass and water. Five herds a month and he's a rich man. And the beef drive idea is catching on all through Texas. Meat prices in the east are out of sight. I know. I just came from there. Cattle raisers are discovering they can market at railheads. And Conroy roams the edges of this—this good, this—progressive enterprise, picking up bits of fallen gold!"

De Puys nodded. "And the drives have to come this way. It's good for the town, Quillen. Where's your civic pride? That's progress. Up the Texas funnel. Why, the local merchants are ecstatic—"

"Yes. The merchants. The almighty dollar. Backed by expert guns. That's a hard combination to beat. But you can't just tromp all over individual rights. Not for long. Everyone in history who ever has, has had cause to witness the power of the little people once they've been stepped on just a little more than they're ready to take. Someone always comes along to lead a common effort."

"And that, I suppose, is your function? Quillen, no good can come of trouble. Why don't you face what's happened, turn to the future? I understand you realized a nice piece of change out of the sale of your stock. Why don't you—"

"Stop," Quillen said. "Just stop. This is no use, I can see. One thing—De Puys, will you investigate that land bill? Will you Send a report to Sheridan outlining the viciousness of it? If you will, I'll take care of the rest. Me, and the men of Two Trees."

The cavalryman sagged visibly. His features slacked and the dragoon mustaches drooped.

"Quillen!" he managed finally. "Are you mad? Do you—" He sat in the chair, unable to speak. Slowly the color mounted in his face. He tried a smile. "You were joking, of course."

"Joking!" Quillen said. "About my land? About the lives lost? I'm dead serious."

"Dead you will be," De Puys muttered, "with that kind of talk."

"You wouldn't like to try it, would you, Captain?" He leaned on the title.

"You're out of your mind," the officer breathed. "You're insane." Suddenly he was shouting, filling the room. "Do you know how long I've been a captain? Do you? Do you realize this occupation duty is my last chance to climb in this service? To the place—the high place—deserved by a De Puys?" He stopped, breathless and red with exertion. "And you say make a report to Sheridan. A report on *my* incompetence. I'll die first!"

Quillen walked to the man, towered over him.

"Then I'll do it for you," he said bleakly.

De Puys waved it aside. "Then do it," he said. "But don't talk to me of reports. Jeb Stuart was in my class. Did you know that?" He brushed vaguely at his face, smoothed the mustaches. "Jeb Stuart! And me a captain. And not only Stuart. Not only him."

De Puys shook his head, turned away.

Coy said, "Captain, I'm leaving tonight for Santa Fe. I'll take the situation to General Sheridan myself. And he'll see me. I'm not a vanquished Confederate. I'm not proud of that fact. But I'll trade on it now. Remember, I gave you a chance to clean up. I'm sorry if it hurts your reputation. But there's too much at stake to worry. I don't fancy your position."

"I do as I'm ordered," the captain said dully. Then, rousing, "Look, Quillen. Bring me some proof. Any proof of wrongdoing. I'll nail Matt Conroy to an anthill. Prove one thing to me and the Army's yours. But don't do this to me!"

Coy peered closely at the officer. De Puys's forehead was dotted with sweat beads, his eyes shuttled.

Quillen grinned suddenly, felt the stiffness in him ease. He turned and strode out, leaving the captain to share the night with his professional conscience.

It was deep dark, plains' fashion, twenty minutes after he left the camp. Coy let the horse pick its easy way along the moonlit road. It was a cold moon, high and pale, obscured from time to time by cloud formations.

When he reached town, Quillen kicked his horse into a trot and clattered down First Street to the square. He reined in by the trees and stared down the noisy, squirming length of Main Street. Shafts of yellow light from doorways illuminated a weird dance as celebrating punchers weaved from place to place. There were gunshots and shouts, female shrieks and the tinny notes of Matt Conroy's piano—the only one in the west of Texas.

Coy shook his head and climbed wearily from the saddle. A little rest would be necessary soon. He could stop on the way to Santa Fe and roll in. His return had played hell with normal hours. He turned his back on the celebration and walked to the pecan tree in the square. The blurred branches and whispering leaves cast an odd serenity over the little park.

"You've made your brag, Quillen," he said aloud. "Now do something about it."

He nodded to himself in the dark and turned. A hard object prodded his back. A gun muzzle. He stiffened and would have spun but the voice stopped him.

"Freeze!" It was a soft voice, somehow familiar. "That's fine. Now back up slowly. That's it. Between the trees. Now turn around."

Quillen did as he was told.

"Just don't do nothin' foolish," the voice said.

Coy peered into the shadow where a tall figure stood, a pistol dangling negligently from one hand. A white slash of teeth in the darkness and the voice came again, more subdued now.

"Didn't aim to startle you," Davey Forrestor said. "Wanted to talk."

"What's the idea of the gun?"

"Didn't know how you'd take to a man creepin' up on you. You ain't exactly popular around here. I figured you might be proddy."

"I'm a Texan, Forrestor. Don't forget it."

"Well, now, *I* won't forget it, Mr. Quillen. Though it seems to me *you* did."

Coy bit back a retort, gazed hard-eyed at the man in the shadows.

"All right, Forrestor. Did you stick a gun in my back to get me over here for an argument?"

Forrestor sheathed his gun. He hunkered with his back to the tree and looked up at Quillen.

"I don't know exactly," he said. "Wanted to talk to you. See how you felt."

"About what?" Quillen squatted near the young rancher. "You know how I feel about Conroy."

"Yeah." Forrestor chuckled. "I sure do. That wipin' his face thing like to killed him. We agree there, all right. I wondered how we stood on doin' something about it?"

"Like what?"

"Ain't but one way I can figure."

"What's your idea? Guns? And ropes hanging from tree limbs? It's been done. See that worn limb up there ?"

He pointed, but the young man ignored the gesture.

"Or would you rather," Coy went on, "have a pitched battle with Conroy's gunhands? In the streets of Two Trees? Now that would be nice. Farmers and kids against Conroy's hired killers. Yes, lots of people might get dead that way—if that's your purpose."

Forrestor's eyes flashed. He stuck a cigarette he'd rolled into his mouth and answered carefully, spacing the words.

"Sounds bad," he said. "Way you put it. Like a lawyer. But I've tried thinkin' around it 'til my head hurt. I don't see no other way."

"And what do you want from me?"

"I don't know, Quillen. I don't know. Except this—I ain't sittin' around while someone steals my land, kills my people, and do nothing! I sorta figured you ought to feel the same way."

He scratched a sulphur match and it sputtered and fizzed, flickering the rough faces of both men.

After a moment Coy said, "I do. And I'm going to do something. But not with bullets."

"Then I'm sorry I wasted your time," Forrestor said, starting up.

"Wait! Hear me out, Forrestor. I'll tell you this once—I'm not afraid to fight. The most satisfying thing I could do right now would be to put a bullet in Harley Maddux."

Davey Forrestor cursed softly through a lungful of smoke. His clean-lined face was rocky in the glow from the cigarette.

"Yes," Coy whispered. "I feel the same. I'd give my other hand to send a ball down his murdering throat! But I can't. I can't because that's personal and it solves nothing. We're only going to have one try, Forrestor. Only one. We have to make it do."

"I hoped you'd say fight, Quillen. I'll tell you why. You see, Kewpie's big and people kinda look up to it. I figured if you'd go, the little men would come and give us a hand." He flipped his cigarette in a long, red arc. "That's all I need. Just a little help."

"You've tried rallying the ranchers?"

"Yeah. No luck. Few are willin'. The ones that need Kewpie water. Conroy won't let 'em touch it. Saves it for the trail herds. We can count on Chub. He's been served one o' them attachments. They're waiting for Holman's next visit to push him. Put a court paper on him."

"These people—you expect they'd come to me?"

The young rancher sighed. "Well, I don't know. They need water. Gonna be a hot summer ... dry. Three days ago I'd a said no. But since the thing in the saloon with Conroy, and the whippin' you put on that fat marshal..." He stopped, turned to Coy. "They might now, sure enough."

Quillen nodded in the darkness. A showdown fight. That would at least clear the air. Then he rose.

"No," he said. "I'm tempted. But it's not good. Too much risk."

"But the reward," Davey said, his face close to Quillen's. "Our land! The country normal; people happy again! What kind of risk is too big for that?"

"Listen," Coy said. "If it was like that, I'd be rolling my battle rig right now. But it's not. And you know it. We kill a few, maybe even all of them—and what happens?"

"The rest run!"

"No! The Army lands on us. Then what have we done?"

"Damn the Army!" the young man said fiercely. "We'll fight them, too! I tell you we got to fight!"

Quillen gripped the man's arm. He shook him sharply. But his voice was soft, in it the recognition of the rage and frustration the young rancher was feeling.

"You know better, Davey," he said. "We kill one trooper— one, mind you!—and Phil Sheridan will roll Case County up like a buffalo hide and drop it in the Canadian."

For a moment the arm was taut-muscled under Coy's fingers. Then the kid relaxed. "Yeah," he said. "Yeah, you're right. But what are we gonna do?"

"Revenge is selfish, Davey, and expensive. In this case, too expensive."

"O.K., Judge," Davey Forrestor said, smiling crookedly. "You sold me. Tell me what to do."

"Fine. Tonight, I leave for Santa Fe."

"Santa Fe?"

"To see Sheridan. After I talk to him I'm sure he'll send an impartial investigator. An Army inspector. If he does that, it's up to us to testify strong enough to cause Conroy and Holman and the rest of the crowd to be prosecuted."

"I just want the Cross-F."

"Sure. And I want my ranch. If you want to get in touch with me, go to Morly's. You know, the doctor's house? If I'm not there, leave messages with Lydia Prinell or her mother. Understand?"

"Yeah. But that Lydia, now. She—"

"Leave that alone, Forrestor." Coy bit the words out.

"Like that, huh?"

They drifted toward the ground-tied mount, cropping grass from the square. Quillen pulled the animal's head up, turned to the other.

"Yes. Like that. You might pass the word around."

"Sure. Good luck, Coy. You want some company to Santa Fe?"

"No. I'll see Paul Angelarry before I go. Then I'll just ride out. No sense in warning them. You keep working on the small ranchers, the farmers. Keep talking, keep the issue hot."

"In case, huh?"

"That's it."

"I saw Angelarry in the Drover's Rest," Davey said, pausing as Coy swung aboard. "He's probably still there. Him and Doc Morly. Watchin' the natives."

He grinned, a young and engaging grin. Quillen gathered the reins. The slim man flicked a careless finger in salutation. Coy hesitated; then leaned down and gripped Davey's hand with his left.

"Thanks, Davey," he said, and kicked the horse into motion.

CHAPTER 10

C OY FOUND the lawyer in the Drover's Rest. He and the portly Morly provided an island of respectability and calm in the midst of such roistering as Coy had never seen. The large room contained a full-fledged rodeo crossed with an election parade. And noise. Music, cheers, screams, and breaking glass; and over it all the deadly serious click of the Big Six wheel, the even drone of deadpan faro boxmen.

"What you're doing is right, Coy," Paul Angelarry said, putting his whiskers close to Quillen's face. "But I don't think it'll do any good."

Quillen downed a drink quickly. "Maybe you're right, Paul. But it's all there is. I'll see you when I get back. Thanks for the money."

He started to turn but stopped, seeing Angelarry bite off a word without utterance. His eyes swung over Coy's shoulder, hung there. Quillen looked around into the soft brown eyes of Matt Conroy. The man had spread himself this night. His black coat was almost knee length and the ruffles in the gleaming white shirt front defied count. It was the first time Quillen had seen him without a hat. Conroy's hair was jet black and appeared soft; it lay easily on the well-shaped head. And the smile was there. Maybe a little wider, more expansive.

Behind Conroy, Moriarty hulked, a suited bull. His pig eyes never left Quillen. But there was no expression in them; his face just sat there on the front of his skull, saying nothing to the world.

At that moment the gun guard shouted from the balcony. Conroy turned, frowning.

"Mr. Conroy," the man cried. He waved, made a motion with his hand like a mock salute and pointed to a door off the top of the stairs. Conroy's face was as close to scowling as Quillen had ever seen it.

"Sorry," Conroy said curtly, moving off. "Business calls."

"Of course," Quillen called after him. "Night is the best time for thieves."

The neat little man kept right on, though he must have heard.

Moriarty materialized in front of Quillen. His eyes were cold. "Don't get smart with Mr. Conroy, huh, cowboy? You hear, cowboy?"

Quillen pushed a rigid finger at Moriarty's swelling chest. "You know what a promise is, ape?" he asked conversationally.

The change of pace confused the hulk; he scowled. "Promise? Yeah," he said, blinking. "Why, hey, cowboy?"

"I made one to myself. A promise to pistol-whip you 'til you beg!"

Moriarty's huge shoulders hunched. Bushy brows drew together and a growl rumbled up out of the man's barrel chest. Quillen reached behind and gripped a bottle on the bartop. He would need the bottle. At least that.

"Moriarty!" Conroy, halfway up the stairs to the balcony, shouted to his man. "Get up here where you belong!"

The ugly look disappeared from the bull's face and he turned in mid-motion like a well-trained horse whose rein had been pulled. He never looked back.

Coy stood looking after Moriarty.

Paul Angelarry chuckled dryly. "You're crazy," the little lawyer said. "But I like you." He patted Quillen's still rigid arm. "Let go of the bottle now—we want to use it."

"On me," Dr. Morly said, beaming over the little lawyer's shoulder. Quillen had forgotten him.

"For the road," Coy agreed.

From Two Trees to Santa Fe was many rough miles of uncivilized and—in some cases—uncharted terrain. Six hundred miles as the crow flies. But Quillen was no crow and before he'd covered ten of those miles his weary body cried for rest. He slumped in the saddle and let the motion of the horse lull him. He drifted in that strange shadowy place between sleeping and waking for a long time.

But his thoughts ran on. This was his own land he traveled now. For more than an hour he'd been riding on his own range. The dust that sifted unseen to his nostrils was Kewpie dust. The realization slipped up on him slowly and shook him from the haze. He looked around. If only it were daylight. His eyes ached for the sight of his home. It had been so long.

January 28, 1861. When the articles of secession had been drafted in Houston the action set off a chain of emotion which rippled outward, covering the state. Sam Houston resigned. Clark, the Lieutenant Governor, took the vacated office and Texas prepared for war. But not all Texans were happy. The state was solid slave; but in truth very few slaves ever labored for Texas masters.

Coy Quillen had been a well-read boy. The sketchy histories and hand-written essays of the period captivated him. And Sam Houston had been an early hero. That, perhaps more than anything, had dictated the difficult course of personal conviction.

Texas went to war. And Coy Quillen went to the North, following his stubborn beliefs. He left a stony-faced father and an unbelieving countryside. Not Coy Quillen, they said. Oh, no! He had gone openly, avowedly to oppose the South's ideals. And people whispered, but they did not shout. Some had never stopped whispering.

Quillen shook himself awake. The horse had stopped. He examined the landmarks and recognized a rising butte silhouetted against the night sky.

"Table Wells," he said and the pony started at the sound.

Coy reined in and surveyed the spot. It was as good a place as any to get some rest. Weariness was deeply seeped into the big frame. He sighed, slid off the still-fresh horse. Two Trees lay a scant ten miles behind. But he needed sleep.

He would be safe enough in the declivity. A natural rise from the depression where the Wells lay shielded him from casual view to the east. A scrub-pine-covered hill stretched upward in the other direction.

Quillen watered the horse, drank thirstily himself. Then he rode through the tight-packed thickets to a cleared space halfway up the western slope. He hobbled the bay and stripped it, pushed the saddle against a tree bole and lay down as he stood. He was hungry. And also tired. Hunger could wait until morning.

But morning never came. Not there.

Five men came. Soundlessly, walking their mounts carefully through the scrub timber. And Quillen, fatigue-drugged and bone weary, had no warning.

He came awake slowly, reluctantly. He'd heard a shod hoof strike rock. Only an overpowering weariness could have made him so careless. Instantly he was aware of danger, but his sticky lids refused to rise. He lay quiet. A horse snorted and stamped.

"He's awake," a voice said, ripping the quiet. "Watch him!"

A saddle creaked. Quillen forced an eye open and tried to focus. He didn't move. It was too late for flight. He waited.

"Well, get him up, Tal. We ain't got all night."

Coy recognized the nasal drawl of Harley Maddux.

"I think we shoot him where he lay, no?"

"Don't think, Lupo," Maddux said. "Just do—Look out!"

Quillen rolled in a sudden burst of speed. His good hand searched his waistband for the gun. But he'd left it in the holster on his right hip. He rolled and his thrashing body struck a horse's leg. The horse reared, squealing. A man cursed and fought the plunging animal.

"Get him!" Maddux shouted, reining up-slope out of the way.

"Don't shoot!" It was a different voice, new. "He can't get away!"

Quillen came to his feet beside the rearing horse. A shadowy man, sitting high in the saddle, fought the excited pony and tried to slash at Quillen with a gunbutt at the same time. Coy grabbed a leg and pulled the man clear of the saddle. The plunging mount struck them and they fell together, rolling into the shadowed underbrush.

A confused shouting arose. The puncher slammed the gun against Quillen's head. Coy grabbed his man, punching, writhing, as they rooted in the darkness.

"Maddux!" the man shouted, struggling in Coy's grasp. He tried to bring his gun to bear and for an instant the cold muzzle touched Quillen's cheek.

Quillen smashed a fist to the man's throat. His left hand groped for the gun, found it, held desperately. The darkness covered the fight. Coy was aware of the movement of horses and man shouts and jockeying for position in the small clearing. He fought savagely, silently. Evil breath blasted into his face as he clamped the man and rolled. A tree stopped them. Coy slammed the bad hand again and again into his opponent's face until the body went limp under him.

"Lupo!" Maddux shouted. "Moriarty! Get him, you fools!"

"I fix, you bet!"

Quillen fumbled the downed man's gun into shooting position. He heard a drumming of hoofs and a shape loomed over him. In one motion he whirled and fired and the horse was riderless instantly.

"Watch it!" Maddux screamed and then everyone was shouting in the darkness.

"Shoot the bastard!"

Coy got his feet under him and thumbed back the hammer of the gun. If only he wasn't so clumsy with his left hand! A slim figure appeared outlined against the paling sky. Quillen's lips drew back and all the resolution never to kill again poured out of him in one cauterizing instant of rage. His finger took up trigger slack.

"Nail him, Bud!" Maddux shouted.

Quillen, a split-hair from shooting, heard the shout and jerked the gun aside. The lead zinged harmlessly into the dirt at the feet of the charging man. Then Bud hurtled into him, fell to the sloping earth.

"Bud!" Coy burst out, twisting under his brother's blows. "Bud, it's me!"

A thudding fist spun his senses and he felt his brother's weight settle on him. Bud hit him again. Coy lifted both arms in an effort to ward off the blows. The boy continued to pound with bony fists. Coy did not try to fight. His brother! His own …

Quillen's mind rebelled and a curious half-coma enveloped him as knuckles tore his flesh and thumped his inert body. His head rolled loosely on the ground.

But he could hear. Strangely he knew what went on, but he could not move or speak. His eyes had closed and the thudding blows of fists and feet were as rain on a high roof. A voice said, "Get off him, hey, cowboy," and a huge hand drew him upright. Coy struggled, tried to resist. But there was no will in him. He felt the rough bark of the tree tearing at his back and Moriarty's merciless fists began to maul him. The man hit like nothing Quillen had ever felt before. The blows jarred and ripped at him.

The night became full of mumbled curses and the whistling breath of effort—but soon there was no pain. Moriarty methodically beat him until his monstrous strength ran out. Then he released Coy's slumping weight and Quillen slid down the tree trunk to the ground.

"Wise cowboy," the hulk wheezed.

"You kill him, huh?"

"Keep your mouth shut, Lupo." Harley Maddux swung down from his mount, walked to the recumbent man. "Very nice, Bud. Conroy will like."

"Yeah," the younger Quillen said. He hunkered against a tree and flopped his head into trembling hands.

Coy nursed a tiny thread of consciousness. There was no reason for him to be alive, let alone conscious. But there it was. A hallway to whereabouts; an awareness that defied reason. He would want to remember this. All of it.

"Lupo! See about Tal," Maddux directed. Quillen sensed the man hovering over him.

"I'm all right," another voice growled. "God! That guy hits like forty rod. Lemme put the bullet in him."

"Wait a minute!" Bud Quillen's voice stopped the action. He stood up. "Conroy said stop him. Not kill him."

"You mind your business, kid," Maddux growled. He pushed back his hat and his white hair glinted in the pale-blue rays of the high moon. "I'll decide what's done in this outfit."

"Look," Bud said, "Conroy said to stop him—keep him from getting to Santa Fe. I heard him. He ain't gonna like it if you go further than that. He's stopped, God knows. He won't go nowhere for a long time. Leave him alone."

"This boy is soft, no?" The Mexican drew his gun. The moon caught the liquid click of the weapon being cocked. "One side. Lupo fix this one."

"You better freeze, Lupo," Bud Quillen said. There was no compromise in his voice. "I said no killin' and that's the way it's gonna be."

Lupo crouched. "You can die too, soft boy," he said and reached around Maddux to level on Bud.

He was too slow. Bud drew his pistol in a fluid motion that caught the men by surprise. He held the muzzle steadily on Maddux's ear, metal touching flesh.

"Tell the Mex to drop it!" he gritted in the foreman's ear. "Tell him!"

Harley Maddux stood stiff and silent. Bud jabbed with the gun and the cold muzzle tore skin.

"All right … all right," Maddux growled. "Put it away, Lupo."

"But, señor—"

"I said put it away!"

"Hey," Tal Everest said. "You gonna stand for that, Harley? Let's get this guy right quick. And his puling brother, too, if that's the way he wants it."

"One move by anyone and you're a dead one, Maddux. Tell 'em that."

There was a tense silence. The night sounds crept up and the movement of tethered mounts was loud for a time. The soft blanket of velvet sleep rolled up in Coy's mind and he fought it back slowly, painfully. If he was going to die, he wanted to know it. When he could focus again through the strange corridor of consciousness, he heard his brother's quiet voice.

"—the way it's going to be. Anybody makes a move toward my brother, I'm shooting you, Maddux. You'll be cold meat before he starts to bleed."

"Don't be stupid, kid."

"No talk. No talk at all. Whatever you're gonna do, do it now. If Lupo lifts that gun, I'll blow you all over the hill!"

"You're making a big mistake, Quillen. You work for Conroy now."

"That's right. Not for you. Now tell these dungrollers to ride or you'll grow a hole!" The soft voice was controlled, even, and there were many things in it—but no fear. No fear at all. And Coy felt a quick pride quite apart from the circumstances. "Move!" Bud Quillen barked.

"All right, boys," Maddux said. "Let's go."

"Not you," Bud said. "Just Everest, Moriarty and Lupo. You stay. We'll ride back together, you and I …"

Maddux said something in answer, but Coy Quillen didn't hear it. Coy Quillen heard nothing at all for some time.

CHAPTER 11

THERE WERE cool hands. That was wrong. Certainly. Coy became aware again behind his lids and lay trying once more to classify his surroundings. He heard sounds now. His nostrils, swollen and thick, detected the smell of food. His stomach twisted. And the hands, soft and cool, darting and smoothing.

"Are you waking finally?" The voice was cool, like the hands, and young. "Mr. Quillen? Are you awake?"

Quillen managed a rattling sigh and the sleep in his throat choked him. He coughed heavily and it hurt. When the pain had dimmed, he rolled his head slowly in the direction of the voice.

"You just lay quiet, sir. I'll get my brother."

"Wait!" Quillen cleared his throat and blinked mightily. His eyes were open, but he could not see. One of them didn't open all the way. It felt thick and soft. "Tell me where I am? Who are you?"

A great blob of white covered each field of vision. On the edges he began to be aware of color and objects. Gradually the girl took form. The sun was behind her and the haze was stubborn.

"Circle," she said. "That's where you are. I'm Patience Miles." Her hands fussed with the blankets, reached up quickly to smooth damp hair off his forehead.

"Circle ..." he mused and remembered.

It had been named that when Hobe Miles settled the rolling hundred acres because Kewpie land surrounded it on all sides. Coy had ridden many times over the poor ranch, hunting yearlings or driving to Tracy, or just out deviling with the boys.

There'd been a son. No, two sons. And a girl. A very little girl, Coy recalled now.

"You've been real bad sick. Three days now. Let me tell Forty and he'll explain—"

"Did you say Patience? That your name?"

"Patience Miles," the girl repeated dutifully. "I'd better go tell Forty—"

"I remember a little girl. Always getting under the horses." He blinked, tried to see. "How'd I get here?"

The girl shook her head. Quillen could see her now. Just a girl. A very pretty girl. He grinned and it was painful. One eye worked very reluctantly.

"Am I alive?" he asked.

"Yes," Patience Miles said. She bent quickly and got a damp rag and applied it tenderly to his face. It felt wonderfully cool. "You lie back. I don't know how you got here, 'cept Forty brought you."

"Forty?"

"He's my brother."

"The other—was it Wilson? Yes. How's Wilson? And your folks?"

The girl took the cloth away. Quillen squinted at the sudden light. She looked at him and blushed for no reason that he could see.

"I'll get Forty," was all she said.

"Forty Miles," Coy mused. His tongue was thick and a very bad taste inhabited his mouth. "Could I have some water, please? Miss—That's pretty awkward. You mind if I call you Patience?"

"Oh, no. No, sir. I don't. You call me Patience." She fussed with her gown, pulling it tight over swelling hips. Her eyes dropped. "I'll get the water."

The room was large and well lit by a glassless window and the wide entrance. The walls were roughly finished and daubed with a white covering. It had flaked here and there. The floor was hard-packed dirt; massive beams ran from sod wall to sod wall and held a collection of hanging items, mostly cured meat and dried skins and hides. Stove in a rear corner. Pots spaced about on it.

A rough camp. But evidences of the girl were many. Brave curtains on a window with no glass; a hooked rug in front of the fireplace. And it was neat.

He sat up. And the pain came. He breathed carefully and pushed away the blankets to examine his body. He was naked. His hard-muscled frame was spotted with blue bruises. A tightly-wrapped cloth circled quite a bit of him.

He touched his face. One eye was puffed and tender and his nose was broken. The passages were blocked. They hurt when he tried to force air through. Both cheeks were scabbed here and there under a ratty growth of beard. He rubbed tenderly and lay back against the wall.

Moriarty and Maddux must have made a good job of the kicks when he'd finally passed out. And Bud. Don't forget little brother. Quillen lay back.

The girl returned with the water, stopped just inside the door. She put the small bucket on a bench. "Here," the girl said.

Quillen took the cup in both hands and got some of the cool liquid into his mouth.

"Better?"

"Yes, Doctor."

She took his hand. The bad hand. Coy watched her face as she examined the bent fingers.

"It's bad, ain't it, Mr. Quillen? The fingers still and all."

"I'm used to it. Don't you bother. I'm obliged to you for patchin' up the rest of me."

"How'd it happen? In the war?"

Quillen sobered. "It's not a pretty story. I've spent a lot of time trying to forget it. There was a fight. In the war. I grabbed a bayonet with my hand." He looked at her, shrugged. "That's all."

"A bayonet—with your bare hand? But why?" Her face was inexpressibly shocked. Quillen laughed.

"To keep from eating it," he said.

And that's the way it had been. Maybe someday he would be able to talk about it. Someday, maybe. But not now.

At that moment the sunlight streaming through the doorway was blocked out. A man stood in the aperture, filling it. Coy twisted on the bunk, shuck mattress hissing with the movement. The girl greeted the newcomer soberly. It was Forty Miles.

"I guess I owe you thanks," Quillen said. He still could not see the man clearly. The sunlight outlined him from behind. "Patience tells me you brought me in."

"This girl talks too much," the figure said and walked into the room. The voice was deep, but the brother was just a boy. A big boy. He carried a milking bucket effortlessly across the room and deposited it on the table. "Patience, get on and do like I told you," the boy ordered.

"We better eat first, you think, Forty?"

"Just git," Miles said and walked to the bunk.

The girl dried her hands on the wisp of apron she wore and hurried out of the soddy. She didn't look at Quillen.

"You feel better?" the boy asked. His voice was a surprising bass rumble. It was odd, a voice so deep with such timbre, coming out of that beardless face.

"Why, yeah, I guess so. I don't know how to thank you. Your sister said I've been here three days."

The boy twisted away and stared stony-faced past Quillen's shoulder. He took off the floppy hat he wore and beat it against his thigh. His clothes were ragged and patched and not too clean, Coy saw. His boots were run-over and the pistol stuck into the waist of the trousers was an antique cap and ball.

"Don't want your thanks, Quillen," the boy said. "I found you on the hillside by the Wells and you was bad hurt. I'd done the same for any critter." He paced to the door like a rangy dog.

"Maybe I wouldn't have brought you here if I'd knowed who you was."

"Why is that?"

"You know why that is. You went against the South. I ain't forgettin' that."

"I see. Well, you're in good company. Everybody around here feels the same way." He closed his good eye, peered with the restricted sight of the swollen one at the red-faced boy. "Including," he added, "Matt Conroy."

The kid stopped. He turned. His eyes slitted. "What's that supposed to mean?"

Coy waved it off. "I'll pay you for your trouble soon as I'm up and around. There's some money in my clothes. Or should be."

"Don't want your money. Just get well enough to get out."

"I'll leave right away," Coy said and swung his legs over the side of the rude bunk.

"Wait a minute!" Forty Miles said, starting forward. "You're too weak."

Coy stopped. The words hadn't stopped him; a blooming nausea doubled him over. "Damn," he said and began falling headfirst toward the floor.

"Jesus!" the kid said and leaped forward. He caught Quillen's heavy body and toppled him back onto the bunk. Coy's ribs screamed a muscular protest. He looked up at the young man, unable to speak for a moment because of the pain.

"Now, look, I didn't mean right away," Forty Miles said. He pitched his hat across the room and pulled a chair to the bedside. "You're welcome to stay here. Patience has gone to town for Doc Morly. When she gets—"

"Wait." Quillen put his hand on the lad's shoulder, fought for control. "The girl—Patience—has she gone yet?"

"She's fixin' to. I hitched up for her."

"Stop her. Don't let her go."

"Stop her?"

"Don't argue, boy! Just stop your sister and bring her back with you."

"Now just a minute, Quillen. This ain't Kewpie. You don't go orderin' me around."

Quillen struggled to rise. Forty pushed him back into the nest of blankets.

"Never mind your damn pride!" Coy gasped. His lungs felt tender, stuffed with cotton; it was hard to breathe. The boy was as stubborn as a frozen cinch. "Trust me, Forty. I'll explain later. Just stop your sister before she leaves for town."

"Why should I?"

"You want Conroy stopped, don't you? Davey Forrestor said you could be counted on." It was just a small lie, Quillen told himself, but it should work. Circle needed Kewpie water to exist—even more than the others.

"Conroy," the boy said. "That son of a bitch."

Coy nodded and relaxed. "Anyway that. Now do like I say, damn it! Get Patience!"

Miles turned away swiftly and leaped out the door. Coy heard his voice raised in a shout. He rolled back into tender exhaustion.

"Make a helluva artilleryman, that kid," he said and pulled the rough blanket up over his nakedness.

Night came. And with it a peculiar chill. In the kitchen of the Miles's soddy a fire was a welcome sight. Its benevolent light reached and flickered, softening harsh lines.

Quillen sat on the bunk propped with a rolled quilt and ate ravenously from a tin dish in his lap. His mouth was raw and each bite sent twinges from sore jaw muscles. Still he forked the fried food purposefully.

"More coffee?"

Coy paused the loaded fork halfway to his mouth and nodded. Forty Miles wrapped a rag around one big sun-darkened hand and dragged the pot away from an open hole in the range. He carried it to Quillen, poured thick aromatic liquid.

"Thanks," Coy said, chewing carefully. " 'Bout time for Patience to get back, isn't it?"

The boy nodded, one side of his face drawn starkly by the firelight, the other shadowed. It was hard to read his expression. A strong face, Coy thought, for all its youth. Forty Miles was eighteen, but he'd been a man a long while. He'd become a man too quickly, like many of those too young to aid the South in her faded cause. They'd been left behind to reap the full harvest of defeat. Forty returned the pot to the range and added a small branch to the fire.

"She'll be along," he said. Then, walking back to the bunk: "You gonna fight, Mr. Quillen? I gotta know."

"Wait'll the others get here, kid." Coy wiped his bad hand across his mouth. "I'll tell you when it's right for you to know."

"But that's why you sent for Davey, ain't it?" The boy unconsciously gripped the black handle of the weapon at his waist. "I really gotta know, Mr. Quillen."

"Wait," Coy said and mopped his plate with a crumbly piece of panbread.

"Wait! That's what I do best—wait. I'm just about waited out."

Coy grinned. He looked at the tall figure pacing with hungry strides. "Forty," he said, "while we're waitin' you could sort of fill me in on what's been happening around here. You know?"

The boy stopped. He walked back to the bunk. "What could I tell you?"

Coy bent his head so the good eye was shadowed from the firelight. "You might start with Conroy. Why do you hate him?"

Miles's head jerked up. The knuckles of one hand popped in the grip of the other. "Why'd you ask that?" he inquired softly.

"Easy, kid." Quillen sipped carefully at the coffee, watching Forty over the rim. "You're proddy on that subject. That's easy enough to see. I want to know why."

"It's none of your put-in, Quillen. You understand that?"

"All right," Quillen said.

Miles turned and Coy could see moist glints at the eyes. He was, after all, only a boy. He took Quillen's plate and sailed it across the room. It clattered against a pot, fell to the floor. Then he walked to the fire and stood, hands clenching and unclenching behind him. Quillen waited. He filled his pipe and lit it, puffing gratefully.

"It wasn't that I was—afraid," Forty said. He faced the fire, his back a taut line. "It wasn't that. I wasn't afraid for myself."

The crackling of the fire became very loud in the room and Coy could hear the stamping of the animals in the corral. He shifted on the bunk and stared at the glowing bowl of his pipe.

"It was just—" The boy started, then shook his head. "She was so young," he said.

"Forty," Quillen said softly, "bring your chair over here. You want to talk to somebody. It had better be me." He. smiled, his sudden transforming smile. "You don't even like me. And it's easier that way."

The boy got the chair and sat beside the bunk, staring dry-eyed at the flickering fire. He stared for a long while before the carefully contained emotions unlocked and the words came. Quillen sucked his pipe and waited, squinting at the cold bowl.

"You know what happened to Dad," the boy said abruptly, not looking at the big man. "And Wilson. You knew Wilson. They both went Confederate—and, well, they both got killed. That left me and Patience with Maw. She was sick, Maw was. Real sick. I worked. But I was just a younker and nobody'd pay me enough to buy medicine and feed us." He snorted, turned away again. "We're twins, you know. Me 'n Patience. Patience and Fortitude. Boy, they sure did name me right. They sure did!" He slammed a big fist onto his knee and left it there, clenched tightly.

"She—your Maw, she died?" Coy prompted gently.

Fortitude Miles shook his blond thatch up and down wearily. "Yeah. Sure. Sure, she died. She died and I lived, and if there's a God, he's a fool!"

CHAPTER 12

THE WAR had ended. Matt Conroy began to make his presence felt in Two Trees and young Fortitude Miles approached him for a job. Conroy hired him, paid him good wages for a boy. He could have had a loyal slave for life. But one day the dapper man saw Patience. The young Patience, lovely and wide-eyed.

Conroy visited Circle. Patience was a pretty girl. And young. But she knew nothing of the world, nothing of men like Matt Conroy. He promised her aid for the family and a better job for the boy. In exchange for what he couldn't find in his own brothels—freshness and acceptance of life without whining. And her woman's body, even then lush and desirable. She'd gone with him in a weak moment.

Coy sucked at the long-dead pipe.

"I should've killed him," the boy said again. "I should've. But I was afraid. Maw died a week after Patience went to town. I tried to get Conroy. I tried. You gotta believe that. But that big fella beat me. And laughed at me."

"Moriarty?"

"Him. Yes. He laughed. And I had a gun and I didn't use it, Mr. Quillen." Forty raised his face and shook his head. "I didn't use it!"

"And you've been living with it ever since," Coy said. "Well, how did Patience get back here?"

"He got tired of her," the boy said. "I guess she wasn't much good to him after Maw died. She died a little bit, too. She just

97

didn't care. Now, she's—well, that's her business, I guess. Hers and Davey's."

Coy looked up. "Forrestor?"

The boy nodded. "They used to be sweet on each other. Everybody thought they'd get married someday. But she won't have him now and he don't know why. If he did I don't suppose he'd want her. It's all a mess!"

Forty sat up abruptly and rose.

Quillen moved carefully under the blanket. He closed his eyes. What could he tell the boy?

Forty stalked out the door. Then Coy heard it, too. The sound of a rolling wagon and horses being pushed. Moments later Davey Forrestor slid out of the shadows and stood blinking in the light of the room. Patience Miles came after him, pulling Lydia by the hand.

Lydia stopped just inside the door. Her eyes grew wide at the sight of Quillen. "Oh, Coy," the girl said and rushed to the bunk.

Her arms clung to him. Coy patted her clumsily. Forrestor stood by the bunk and looked down at them, thin face impassive in the flickering firelight.

"You sent for me," he said harshly. "I'm here."

"I see," Quillen said, sensing strain in the man. He pushed the girl away. "Sit over there," he directed, pointing. "I have business."

"You had business three days ago," Davey Forrestor said. "In Santa Fe."

"Easy, Davey. They jumped me. Maddux, Moriarty—the whole bunch."

Forrestor snorted, moved forward. "Without killing you? I find that a right tough cud to chew. Everybody's talking about how bad they want you dead. Now that you're the messiah—the Moses of Two Trees."

The slim puncher dragged up a chair, straddled it. His eyes never left Quillen and his set face did not relax. "Yes, sir. I find that right hard to believe."

Coy looked at him levelly. Neither gaze wavered. Forty entered the room, stood quietly in the background.

Quillen finally spoke, his face a mask. "Believe what you like," he said. "As I do about you."

"Now what do you mean by that?" Forrestor asked softly. His right hand moved a trifle.

"I find it a mite hard to believe Conroy would know where to find me"—he paused—"seein' as how I told nobody but you."

Forrestor slammed out of the chair. His gun leaped into his hand and centered Quillen. "Damn you!" His finger tightened on the trigger.

Quillen smiled. Big, like someone had said something very funny. It hurt his face and for a rock-hard instant he was afraid the angry man would shoot. But the smile was enough.

The gun muzzle dropped a hair. Coy relaxed and settled back against the quilt. His hands were wet.

"Sit down, Davey," Quillen said. "I found out what I wanted to know. And it was important. Now we can get down to business."

"Man, you hadn't oughta—what business?"

Quillen squinted up at the tall puncher. The firelight cast a shadow behind him on the wall. It seemed to fill the room.

"Fighting business," he said levelly.

Davey Forrestor shook his head back and forth slowly. He slid the gun back into the holster tied low on one slim flank. A grin crept into his eyes and finally bent the mouth corners.

"You're a pure fool," he drawled, pushing his hat back on snarled hair. "I almost shot you."

Coy nodded. "I hoped you would."

"Shoot you?"

"No," he said solemnly. "I hoped you'd almost." He looked up. "I had to find out. And now we fight. That's what you wanted, isn't it?"

The young man bit his lip. "You know it is. But I don't see …"

"All right." Quillen twisted on the bunk, called to the girl. "Lydia. I want you to go into town."

"I'll go, of course, Coy." She glided to the bed, smiled down at him. Her hand flattened and moved with a kissing touch over his battered features. "Why don't you wait, Coy? Until you're stronger. Your face is kind of beat. You need rest."

Quillen grasped her hand and held it for a moment. Over Lydia's shoulder he saw Forrestor gazing at the Miles girl; Patience was puttering at the stove, palpably ignoring him. The young rancher's face held the puzzled, hurt look of a male who tries to understand his woman. Quillen pulled gently on Lydia's arm until she was sitting on the bunk. He looked for a long time into her eyes.

"Just a little while, Lyd," he said for her ears alone. "Not long. We have a thing to do. Now is the time to act. And I have to help."

"Whatever you say, Coy." The girl's eyes filled suddenly and she rested her head against his bare chest.

The quiet was loud for a time. Then Forrestor coughed and fumbled for the chair he'd flung. He dragged it up closer to the bunk and straddled it again. The posture suited him. He crossed corded forearms on the chair's back and dropped his chin to rest on them. His eyes were somber. Quillen watched him over the girl's bent back.

"Lydia," Coy said finally, "I can't send Forty to town because he doesn't know Paul and it will be very late when you get there. Are you listening?"

Lydia sat up. Patience Miles hurried over from the stove and handed her a piece of cloth. She dabbed at her eyes and nodded.

Coy squeezed her hand and addressed Forrestor. "How many men can we count on, Davey?"

"Well, that's a hard thing to say."

"Make a guess. Hurry up."

"Right now, way things stand—about a dozen."

"A dozen. Conroy's got that many in town. And God knows how many more at Kewpie."

"Eighteen," Forrestor said.

"Does that include Maddux and that Mex? And Everest?"

"No," Davey said. He turned his eyes away. "Doesn't include your brother either. They all belong to the Honor Guard!" He groped for makings, began shaping a cigarette.

Coy tapped his hand on the side of the bunk. He couldn't let Bud influence him in this. One way or the other. He blew out his breath, started to speak.

"Look," Davey interrupted, expelling smoke. "Don't worry about them. Conroy's gunhands. When the time comes, we'll do all right. What you got in mind? And how come we talk fight now and the other night you said it was the last thing we could do?"

Quillen sat up. "I'll tell you. First, I want to get Lydia started."

"But what are we going to do?"

Quillen looked at the younger man. In the light of the dying fire the scene was eerie, unreal. He raised his hand. "We hit 'em," he said, evenly. "And then we hit 'em again. Hard and dirty and often. That's all."

Lydia straightened, moved away on the bunk. "I'm ready whenever you say, Coy."

"Good. Take the best horse and ride like hell. When you get to town don't let anyone know where you came from. Find Paul," Coy went on. "Bring him right out here. Don't wait for anything and don't spend all night explaining. You tell him I'll lay it out for him when he gets here. Got that?"

Lydia nodded and rose.

"Before you come back," he added, "stop at the stable and get the best horse available for Forty. Buy it. Paul will help you pick one and give you the money. Now, git."

Davey Forrestor turned to Quillen as the girl disappeared into the night. He sucked the end of his cigarette to glowing brightness and spoke through a cloud of smoke.

"You know, Coy, I been wanting a crack at Conroy for a long time. Now—" He shook his head, shrugged. "Maybe wanting ain't gonna be enough. Seems like all we got is want."

"You're right. It isn't enough. But whatever we need, we'll get."

"One thing," the slim puncher said. "What changed your mind?"

"About fighting?"

"About fighting. You made a pretty good case to me there in town. About the military and steppin' on Sheridan's corns and all that tumbleweed. What about the Army now? Gettin' slammed around changed your tune, didn't it?"

Coy smiled at the intense young man. He leaned back, suddenly very tired. "Yes," he said, "I guess it did. But not like you think, Davey. Not like you think at all."

"What do you mean?"

"I told you revenge was selfish. I meant it. No, it's just that now I'm not worried about the soldiers. Not any more."

"Not worried? But why? What made it any different?"

"When Lydia gets back with Paul Angelarry, I'm going to take a precaution to make sure we don't have to worry about the cavalry at all."

Davey flipped his stained cigarette stub at the fireplace. He leaned forward.

"This I gotta hear, 'cause if you can take care of the Army"— he paused, one hand sliding to the black pistol on his hip—"we can take care of Conroy. We sure can."

CHAPTER 13

IT WAS simple to him. But he had a hard time convincing his audience that the danger of the Army stepping in when they made their play against Conroy was nil.

By accusing Davey of selling him out to Conroy, Coy had chinked the only possible hole in his theory. He had told three people of his impending visit to Santa Fe. Then he'd been stopped on the way. Someone had told Conroy. Coy knew that Paul Angelarry hadn't told anyone of their plan. It was not his way. And now he was sure of Forrestor. That left only one.

"You see," Quillen said for what seemed to him the tenth time, "De Puys can't afford to use the troops. He is personally responsible. As a man. Not as a commander. Soldiers do as they're told. But they won't misuse people at the whim of an officer. Soldiers are people, you know. Even if they're Union. Now if De Puys tries to interfere in our fight with Conroy—well, what good would he be without his troops?"

Davey Forrestor sighed. "Coy, I—well, maybe I'm thick. But I just plumb don't understand. What guarantee have we got we don't get jumped by the Army in the middle of a dogfight with the Conroy bunch? And it'll be awful close."

"All right," he said. "One more time. There's only one way the bunch could have known I was riding out to Santa Fe. De Puys. He was the only one I told that I'm not sure of. And later in the Drover's Rest Conroy was called away. It was De Puys. Had to be. They knew what my mission was and they were afraid I might be heard. So I had to be stopped. When they jumped me, it was sup-posed to be all day for Coy Quillen. Bud stopped that."

"That means De Puys is in on it," Patience Miles said. "An army officer."

"Yes. What the deal with him and Matt Conroy is, I don't know. Maybe we won't ever know. Anyway, he can use the power of his office of military governor only as long as he can put a good face on what he does. Like the manifestoes. He can claim ignorance of law and get away with it. But he can't order his troops into a fire fight with us and make them buy just any story."

Forrestor scratched a match in the sudden quiet, fired his cigarette deliberately. The flaring sulphur stick carved his lean features into a mask of hard strength.

"What you mean is," the slim puncher said slowly, "De Puys'll be afraid to try to enforce them funny laws of his with any action that'll bring someone from Santa Fe."

"Of course. Now you've got it. He won't know that by the time we get in the thick of whatever kind of battle they make us fight, Forty here'll be in Santa Fe, with a petition to General Sheridan for an investigating officer."

Forty Miles stirred in his chair. He rubbed a boot on the floor and spoke apologetically, "How come me, Mr. Quillen? I can shoot a gun. Why don't you send someone else?"

"No, Forty. You'll go." Coy sank back into the folded quilt and slumped painfully. He opened his eyes after a moment, smiled at the boy. "You're the best man for the job."

"One thing, Coy," Davey Forrestor said. "What if we figured it wrong? What if De Puys really ain't in on the crooked dealin' and pulls the troops into it? What then?"

Quillen looked at Davey for a long time. No one spoke.

"I'd like," he said, speaking slowly, carving out each word with care, "to say nothing... that we fight on. But that's not the way it is. The first soldier we shoot, we're done. That'll buy us just a whole hell of a lot more than we can handle. That's all. I know Phil Sheridan. He'd burn Case County like a torch."

"Then we're taking a long chance…"

Coy nodded. "A real long one. But it's better than no chance." He looked around. "I'm ready."

"So am I," Forty Miles said, rising from his chair.

"And me," Patience interjected. "If there's anything I can do."

Quillen took her hand with his and pressed it against his leg. Davey chewed on his lip, looking at the girl. Then he straightened slowly, a reckless grin growing on his face. "I hope I do better than the last time," he said.

"You will," Coy promised. "This time you'll be backed by metal. In the hands of men with purpose. It makes all the difference."

"Now all we got to worry about is gettin' the rest of the men to go along."

"I thought you said they were ready? That they'd follow me?"

Forrestor nodded slowly, stood up fingering his hat. "I said I thought so," he drawled. "I still do. But I won't find out for sure 'til I've talked to some of them farmers and small ranchers over east." He pushed the hat on with a quick gesture. "But if they don't go along … I'm gettin' Maddux."

Quillen sat up, ignoring the quick twinges of pain from his sore ribs. He shook his head slowly, peering at the tall young man.

"I know," Davey said. "Revenge is selfish." There was a sudden movement and his hand appeared at hip level filled with Colt .45. A grim little smile played on his lips. "I know what you say is true, Coy. And I know what my heart says, too."

Quillen looked quickly to the girl. Her back was turned to the men, but Coy saw small movements of her head as she muffled her face in her apron.

"All right," he said. "You go now and get a meeting set up. I'll talk to the men. If they go along, fine. If they don't … we'll do what we can with what we've got. Good enough?"

The grin came back. Davey slid the .45 into the holster, slapped it. "Keno," he said.

"Meanwhile," Coy went on, "I'll get Forty started to Sheridan. Soon's Paul gets here and draws up the petition. Tomorrow I'm getting up to do a little shooting. You wait'll night to come back."

"A little shooting? You figure on bein' a little selfish your ownself, maybe?"

Coy lifted the bad hand, looked at it a long time. He moved the thumb up and down; the fingers didn't move at all. "Got to practice," he said. "Got to stretch my arm."

The flat crack of the Henry rolled in the ravine. The report hissed out over the jagged lip and sang across the stretching plain. A wooden slab, propped on the bank, jerked with the sound. A round hole appeared next to a rude X chalked on the wood. Coy straightened from a shooting crouch and peered at the target.

"Low," he muttered. "A damn sight too low." He hefted the rifle in his right hand, twisted it 'til the stock came against his left hip. Then he glued his eyes to the piece of wood, slid his left hand to the grip and touched the trigger with a probing finger. This was the hard part. Coming to know a familiar weapon from the other side of your body. His left forefinger, the trigger finger, hadn't yet gotten the feel of touching off a shot.

Quillen turned away from the target. Then he whirled back, came around, fired. The slab jumped. A round hole had cut off one arm of the X.

Coy grinned. He hoisted the rifle, sighted at low-marching clouds in the hard blue sky. His shoulder twinged with the move-ment and he remembered the days of pain. His ribs were still wrapped, but only occasionally did the pain come.

He grimaced and glanced eastward toward the Miles's ranch. A hogback blocked the view. Patience probably couldn't even hear the shots this far away. Coy turned back to the target and levered a round into the chamber.

A stringy jack-rabbit poked its nose around a scrub pine fifty yards up the arroyo. The small animal hopped into the draw and sat, peering at Quillen with bright beady eyes. Coy shifted the rifle. The jack tensed.

"Sitting," Coy murmured. "Won't prove nothing that way."

He dropped the barrel and fired into the dirt and the rabbit was off and running up the draw before the smoke curled. Coy slipped his hand in practiced motion from the grip, caught the lever with his thumb, racked it both ways, touched trigger. The bounding rabbit crumpled at the lip of the ravine.

Quillen watched the still body for a long moment. He patted the stock of the Henry and nodded. "Good enough," he said.

He had two hands again. Or a substitute, at least. He recalled how he had come to think of the trick of binding the rifle in his bad hand and firing left-handed.

His gun battery had been given another noncom when he was wounded. Quillen had been confident he could get it back. The lieutenant disabused him quickly. He was assigned to forge and forage when he came back from the hospital.

"Coy, you're a good man and my senior noncom to boot," Lieutenant Symonds had said. "But ain't no one-handed man alive can swing a trail or lock on a spoke and heave. You take the forge wagon."

So Quillen forged and foraged.

Then he found a saber. For weeks he experimented with different methods of binding the wicked blade to his right hand. Finally a combination of rawhide and linen gave him a solid binding which made the saber an extension of his still-solid right arm. That day he challenged the lieutenant to a saber duel and beat him. The officer gave him back his battery.

And now, in the sapping heat of the Texas noon, the memory gave him back his hope. If he could bind on a saber and fight a battle, he could certainly learn to fire a rifle from the wrong side.

Coy wiped his sweaty hand on faded blue pants and started back to the Miles's place. He hadn't brought a horse, preferring the muscle-stretching walk after days of inactivity.

Dust puffed up under his boots in yellow clouds. His eyes, squinted against the peeling sun, searched the surrounding terrain with habitual thoroughness. He found himself thinking of Lydia. So beautiful, so eager to please him. Maybe a little too eager. He frowned with the thought and swung the dangling rifle against his leg.

A shot rang out somewhere ahead. He stopped, listened intently. From the direction of the soddy. Patience was there alone. Quillen broke into a run up the canyon, pushing loads into the Henry as he went.

It had to be trouble. Coy ran faster, the exertion punishing his sore body. He grabbed for air, pounded on. At the hill just before the house, he paused and took stock. No sense in running into ambush. His gaze traveled the ridge-top. Nothing in sight. He wiped sweat from his eyes and started around the hill at a trot.

When he judged himself to be directly behind the Miles's homestead, he began angling up the sloping hill. The grass deadened the sound of his boots, but it made the footing uncertain. Quillen reached the top and crouched there, peering into the ranchyard below.

His breath came painfully and for a moment his eyes refused to identify the activity they found. Then he sorted impressions and the impact hit him like a shout in a small room.

Horses milled around a group of figures in the beaten area by the front door. Patience Miles, naked and struggling, twisted in the grasp of the Mexican, Lupo. A laugh, ugly and full of male triumph, drifted up the slope. Three other Conroy men stood around and shouted encouragement.

As Quillen watched, unable for the moment to act, the girl screamed and fell backward to the hard ground. Lupo fell on top of her. The soft body thrashed and dust swirled, obscuring the struggle.

CHAPTER 14

QUILLEN jacked a cartridge into the Henry, gripped it for shooting. He filled his lungs and leaped out over the ridge-top, screaming like a race of fiends.

The group by the soddy stiffened with the first shrill whoop and turned. All but Lupo. The girl heard the shout, the following shot, and threw her legs around the man, pinning him. One ragged puncher with a flamered bandanna at his throat saw Quillen racing toward them and lit out around the soddy. Another dropped with Coy's first shot. He lay unmoving. Tal Everest, the remaining watcher, dropped to one knee and coolly fired his pistol at the onrushing man.

All this Quillen saw as he ran shouting down the slope. A part of his mind stood off and classified the men and the action; another worked the lever of the Henry with precision and no loss of motion. Everest's second shot buzzed off the rifle's stock. Quillen shook with the impact. His pounding legs drove him on.

He snapped a shot at Everest, saw the man wince as the ball tore a furrow in his cheek. Coy racked the Henry as he reached the level yard and stopped, sliding in the silky dust. For just a moment there was no sound. Behind Tal Everest, Quillen could see Lupo, struggling to pull away from the girl's entangling limbs. And then he was too busy staying alive to think.

"It's Quillen!" Everest shouted.

The puncher behind the soddy opened fire. Tal Everest rolled and came up running. Coy threw a shot at him and missed. He ran on toward the horses untouched. Coy danced forward a few steps, dropped to one knee. His eyes searched the house corner. A gun appeared. Then a bearded face framed by a red cloth. Coy fired. A thin scream, stopped abruptly, hung in the sunlight. The puncher tumbled into sight, limp.

"Lupo!" Tal Everest, mounted now and circling, trying to control his spooked horse, shouted to his remaining henchman. "Get out o' that!"

Quillen leveled on Everest. The man's horse came down in a crow-hop and Coy fired, missed. He cursed, got to his feet. He ran doggedly, tired now, toward the horseman. Everest called once more to the Mexican and fled, flogging the bay into a dead run down the cart-track.

Quillen turned to Lupo. As he did, the girl screamed. Coy levered the Henry and stalked the Mexican who, having shaken the girl, climbed to his feet and was trying to claw forth his pistol.

"Pray to somebody, you bastard," Coy hissed. "Pray!" And pulled the trigger.

But the rifle did not fire.

Lupo, erect now, dust-covered and wild-eyed, saw the hammer fall and no shot come. His bearded face split in an evil grin. "Tu Diablo!" he spat and raised his gun. "Y su Madre!"

Coy was five feet from the pistol muzzle when the shot came. When the rifle had missed fire, he hadn't wasted precious seconds attempting to unjam it. It would have been no use and he knew it. Instead, he forced his numb legs to drive forward in a vain hope of closing with the man.

The shot should have torn him in two. Lupo fired from the hip with great deliberation. And Quillen, already beginning a vicious swipe with the rifle, tensed against the blow. But the bullet hissed harmlessly over his head as Patience Miles hit Lupo's legs from behind.

Quillen pulled away in a savage grunt as he saw the man stumble. His powerful arm swung through and the tough rifle stock crushed against facial bone. Coy spun all the way with the blow and struck again as he came around. Then he lost sight of everything but the evil face and he pounded and slashed, stabbing the gunbutt into the features of the fallen man, mixing flesh with dust and blood with bone.

Patience stopped him finally. She tugged at his straining arm, sobbing and pleading, and—after a time—Coy heard her. He stood weaving, shaking the haze from his head. The girl clung to him and he turned, stumbling over the remains of Lupo. The rifle dragged at his suddenly weary arm. He tried to throw it away. He could not. It was part of him now. Bits of hair and blood stuck to the stock.

"Mr. Quillen, Mr. Quillen," the girl said, sobbing it, over and over.

"Easy, Patience. Easy now, honey."

His breath came easier now and the sweat no longer ran in streams down his tight face. He held the girl against him and relaxed in the free feeling of spent passion.

"Patience," he said. "Patience, see if you can quit crying long enough to tell me what happened." He ran his hand over her trembling shoulders. Her skin was like hot velvet under the film of dust.

Patience Miles was a mess. A beautiful, naked mess. Her only covering was one dun-colored stocking which somehow had clung to its place in all the struggle. Her hair, filled with dust and muddied with sweat, was snarled and straggled in all directions. Tear tracks traced moist passages through the dust on her cheeks. She shrugged away and stood gazing at him. He said nothing. She covered her breasts with her arm and waited, head bent.

Coy licked his lips, looked away from her. Bodies on the ground; dead vultures at Circle. "Patience, I've got to go," he said. "This means we'll have to start now. Tal Everest knows me. He'll tell Conroy where I am."

"But they know already! That's what they came for. For you."

"Let's go inside," he said. "If they came here for me, we have no time to waste. No time at all."

It was cooler in the soddy. And dark. The girl scurried to the corner where her bunk was. Coy dropped into the hide-covered armchair facing the door. The rifle, still bound to his hand, bumped on the floor. Quillen sat limply. Now the fat was really in the fire.

He heaved himself erect in the chair. The girl had slipped a dress over her nakedness. She was still a mess. Quillen smiled. "You're a mess," he said.

"Yes, sir. I guess I am." She pointed at the gunbutt. "Please wipe that off."

He looked at it. There was no feeling in him. He brushed the bloody stock carelessly on his pant-leg.

"Listen to me, Patience," he said. Her eyes had followed the rifle stock. He pulled it away from her gaze. "I can't take it off," he said. "It's tied. And I need it. Now listen…"

"Mr. Quillen, I can't—"

"You listen," he barked. She stiffened, stepped back from him. "It was bad. All right. But it's done. Now think about the others. About Forty, halfway to Santa Fe. Lydia, collecting guns. All the people of—"

"I'll try," she said weakly. "What shall I do?"

"I'm leaving, Patience. But I'm not running. Just getting out of sight. Now here's what you do. Find Davey. I know that's a big order, but there's no other way. You tell him to meet me at the Kiowa Fault… where the Tracy road crosses."

"The Fault…" The girl hesitated, moved forward slightly. "But that's where the Army camp is."

Coy rose. He nodded, walked to the door and glanced out. "It's almost an hour past noon," he said, returning. "Tell Davey to wait until deep dark. And get this, Patience—tell him to bring a strong wagon and a four-horse team."

"A four-horse team. Yes, sir, Mr. Quillen."

He moved to the door, carrying his coat and saddle in the unencumbered hand. He spoke over his shoulder. "If you see Lydia, tell her not to worry."

"I will."

Patience had smoothed her hair and tried to brush some of the dust away. Her feet were bare. He thought to thank her for the treatment he'd received and the hospitality. But the words wouldn't come. The girl stood calmly under his scrutiny, seemed to know his thoughts.

"Mr. Quillen," she said, real soft, "I'll find Davey for you." A faint smile came and went away. "You just bet I will."

"Find him for yourself, Patience," he said. "Even if you tell him, he'll understand—now."

The sun had risen almost straight overhead. Coy squinted at it, turned to Patience, who had followed him outside. She rubbed her bare feet in the dust. Five feet away, the dead Mexican lay. Flies buzzed busily. In the hot red sky, a lazy wing-shape looped, hovering.

"Mr. Quillen," the girl said again. She moved to him, looked up, dust-streaked face solemn and contained. "I'm right grateful you got here when you did. I reckon I been used enough."

The smile slipped from his face. He dropped the saddle, slid the black hat onto his head. Quillen looked at the ragged woman, standing in the wreckage of her world, unafraid and strong.

"Yes," he said, breathing it. "I reckon we all have."

CHAPTER 15

QUILLEN shifted in the unfamiliar saddle and glanced at his back-trail. No movement. He hadn't seen another human since leaving the Miles's soddy. At the last moment he had left his own split McLelland to take the horse and hull of one of the dead men. There had been three to choose from.

He nudged the horse into a rocking trot. Night was approaching over the rim of the Ran-Toms and he was still a ways from the cavalry post.

The large form of Sergeant Eldred O'Bain made quite a blotch on the side of the cantonment tent. When Quillen slid through the flap, the cavalryman looked up in surprise.

"Coy Quillen! By the fates that dog us," he said. "Come in, lad. Come in."

The tent was large, lighted by a hanging candle-lantern. There were two bunks against the side walls. A rifle rack by the centerpole held two sabers and a pair of carbines. Lockers and military paraphernalia lay about. The floor had been pounded and was clean as a puncheon kitchen. Coy glanced over his shoulder, moved to the solid sergeant.

"I haven't much time, Red," he said. "I've got more things to do than I have time to do them in."

"Of course, boy. Come in and sit. Here, on the stool."

Quillen hesitated. "The flap," he said. "Could I ..."

"Drop it then, if it'll make you feel better. I heard the devil's own had marked you. I didn't think you'd let it frighten you."

Quillen turned from the closed flap, grinned at the violent O'Bain. He walked to the stool, sat with a tired sigh. "Not Conroy I'm afraid of, O'Bain."

The sergeant put aside the field desk he'd been holding across his thick knees and wiped his hands on yellow-striped pants. His shock of red-gray hair glinted with the candle's flicker.

"Isn't it now," he said. "Then what're you creepin' and duckin' for? Is it the Army you be fearin'?"

"O'Bain, did you hear of the ambush Conroy laid for me?"

"I heard, lad." The Irishman's eyes slid away. " 'Twas your brother, it's said in town."

Coy nodded. "Him. And others. Maddux and Lupo —well, never mind them. They tried and they failed. Now it's time to strike."

"Strike? Would you be talkin' insurrection, Quillen? In the face of a Union soldier?"

"Wait now. Wait. You know how I feel about violence. About men using force to further their own petty ends. But the time has come to determine whether law is right—or might. And because of the Army—yes, because of the very guidon you follow—there is no other way but to fight!"

"You're daft, man." O'Bain rose abruptly and strode to the back of the tent. "You can't be serious. Why, one shot—one, mind you—against Conroy, one drop of blood, and I'll be leadin' the troop on your trail. Don't make it be like that, Coy Quillen. Don't spread blood across the territory."

"The blood is spilt already, Red. There's no turning back."

"De Puys," the big sergeant said, coming into the light. "De Puys will hang you, Coy, if you've touched a man of that jackal pack."

Quillen looked up. His lips pulled away from his teeth in what was supposed to be a smile. "I killed three of them twenty miles from here this afternoon. At Circle."

"Virgin preserve us," O'Bain muttered, unbelieving.

"And one more thing, Red." Quillen stood, faced the agitated sergeant. "Conroy's a dog in the open. His partner is another breed entirely and you know the other very well. His name is Peter De Puys … may his manhood rot on a hot rock!"

O'Bain moved slowly to the bunk, sank down upon it His eyes were tight at the corners. The big head drooped tiredly. "Tell me, lad. Tell it slow and tell it all."

As he recited the story, Quillen felt pity for the sergeant who had given his life to an ideal. And contempt for the man who had been the instrument of making that gift a mockery. The sergeant believed him. He had to.

"Quillen," O'Bain said when his quiet rage had spent itself, "I know what you want, of course. When you start in on Conroy, you'll be wanting to know the cavalry won't be ridin' up your neck."

"That," Coy agreed, "and something else."

"The dog," O'Bain said, not hearing. "The dirty damned hound of a man! I must believe you, Coy Quillen. It fits. All of it, more's the pity. And this I'll do. I'll see the boys know the truth. I'll tell them of our officer's perfidy. If I can keep from killing him myself!"

Coy moved to the flap. "If one soldier tries to stop us, we'll throw down our arms. That, I promise, O'Bain. Conroy, De Puys, Moriarty—the rest … they're fair game."

"And Maddux?"

Coy smiled. He lifted the tent-flap. "Whatever happens, Harley Maddux is a dead man." He glanced out. "It's deep dark. I've got a man with a wagon near here."

"A wagon?"

"The farmers and small ranchers have no weapons. Not weapons to stand up to the Conroy crowd. Muzzle loaders and cap-'n-ball pistols." He shook his head, smiled at O'Bain, who had begun to get the implication. "We can't fight with pitchforks, Red."

"You're asking me …"

"No. I'm not asking you to do anything. Just don't be too quick to investigate any strange noises in the vicinity of the orderly room."

"Good luck. I should have known you'd think of the Henrys. Son of a bitch! You might as well put them to use. We've never had the firing of them."

"O'Bain …"

"Don't say it, Coy Quillen. It's our own dictates we each be followin'." The cavalryman's voice dropped in volume, became a low rumble. "A man's land is reason to fight. Aye, maybe it's the only reason worth a damn."

Coy looked at the big Irishman. He cleared his throat. There was nothing to say.

"Be careful, Quillen," O'Bain whispered.

"I will."

There was a noise outside the tent. The flap was thrown back and De Puys stepped through. "Sergeant O'Bain," the fat officer said. "Place that man under arrest." He pointed a finger at Quillen. The other hand held a gun.

Quillen stiffened, locked his muscles as the shock rode him. All he could think was that Davey and the rest would be waiting—depending on him.

"You're a foolish man, Quillen," De Puys said. "A fugitive from justice and you come here." He shook his head and stepped further into the tent. "I told you to place the man under arrest, Sergeant. Did you hear the order?" The command bite had crept into the little man's tone. He held the pistol steadily. "Or are your sympathies with this turncoat … this muddler in the waters of people?"

"I see you changed your tune, De Puys," Quillen said, playing for time. O'Bain had as yet made no move. "Once you told me you never meddled in the affairs of local officers. Jurisdictional, you said."

The dragoon mustaches twitched, rose at opposite angles. "Unless requested, Quillen. Remember? Unless requested."

"What's the charge?"

De Puys smiled. The little pig eyes gleamed and the feverish look Quillen had seen once before came over the captain's face. "Assault will do. There's a matter of beating the marshal."

Coy relaxed. The captain hadn't yet found out about the fight at Circle. He still had a chance.

"De Puys," Coy said, turning slightly so his good left hand was toward O'Bain, "what makes you think Conroy won't double-cross you when the dirty work is over?"

"Conroy? I have nothing to do with Conroy. You're out of your senses, boy." He turned to O'Bain without taking his eyes from Quillen. The gun remained firm. "Sergeant! Must you be invited to follow orders? Place this man under arrest."

"He has no gun, sir," the sergeant growled, moving slowly.

"Search him and see, O'Bain. You've been in the Army long enough not to take anything for granted."

"Yes, sir. But no gun, sir."

Coy twisted as O'Bain brushed him. The sergeant's pistol holster, flap open, thrust up as the soldier bent to inspect Quillen's boots. Coy reached out, plucked the heavy pistol out of the holster. In the same movement, he shoved O'Bain roughly against De Puys.

De Puys's gun went off.

Coy dived for the floor.

"Look out, you fool!" De Puys screamed. "Get out of the way!"

Quillen twisted on the hard-packed earth, snapped a shot at the hanging lantern. Glass broke and the candle fell, burning 'til it hit the floor. Then he rolled. A gun boomed in the darkness. De Puys shouted. O'Bain, apologizing and stomping around the captain, gave Quillen enough time to roll out under the loose side of the tent.

The camp stirred and muttered. In ten minutes, it would be in an uproar. A single bugle chattered, trailed off. Quillen ran to where he'd left his horse. They would be searching as soon as De Puys could get the men organized. He slammed into one trooper, ran on cursing loudly at the man. The picket line was a welter of confusion. Coy slipped through the disturbed horses, found his own behind the hay tent. Untying the animal, he slapped it, sent the horse galloping into the lake of shadows that was the south plain. He ducked low, dodged a guard patrol and ran in the opposite direction. He had only a short way to go.

The Kiowa Fault was an unexplained gouge in the relatively flat plateau. It ran from near the Red River almost fifty miles, meandering here and there without apparent geological reason. The Tracy road dipped downward sharply where it crossed the Fault, the lips on both sides having been worn by countless hoofs and iron-banded wheels into a gentle slope that fell away into the twenty-yard-wide declivity. It resembled a dried-up river bed where, so scholars declared, no river could ever have been.

Quillen found it without incident after having fled the aroused camp. His breath came shortly and his aching ribs, still sensitive from his beating, bothered him. He rested for a moment at the bottom of the Fault.

He rose. Forrestor would be waiting. He strode down the cut, walking swiftly and surely in the bright moonlight away from the Tracy road.

Forrestor stepped out from behind a jutting rock before Quillen had walked fifty feet. The slim rancher hefted his drawn gun, grinned tiredly.

"Howdy. Heard you a while back. Wanted to make sure it was you."

"You got here," Coy said, moving toward the man. "You got here, so you know about …"

The smile went. The young puncher's lean face lengthened and tightened. He jerked his head once. "I heard. I'm owin' to you, Quillen. If that bastard had hurt that girl ..."

"It's done. Let it lie." Coy looked around. "Where's the wagon?"

"It's here. Around there." Davey swept a hand behind. "But wait. Let's get evened up on what's happened. You tell me, I'll tell you."

"Somebody at the wagon?"

"Chub Willets," Davey said. He squatted, took out makings. "Smoke? Oh, yeah—that hand."

Quillen flopped on the ground beside the young man. "People ready?"

Davey waited just a fraction, then nodded. He scratched a match, lit a cigarette. He passed it to Coy, started building another.

Quillen took the thin cigarette. "You have any trouble, Davey?"

"Might as well be honest, Coy—I had a heap. Folks want to fight. Always have. Some of 'em will, too. And don't fault 'em 'cause they ain't jumpin' in the middle of this thing without lookin'. They're good people. All of 'em."

"I know they are, Davey." Coy studied the tiny glow of his cigarette. "What was wrong? Me?"

"Some," Forrestor admitted. "But not all. I got 'em to promise to meet at Chub's place. Chub, now, he'll fight. Give him a chance to dig spurs into Conroy and he'll ride a wildcat. And there's ..."

"How many, Davey?"

The question was softly asked. The young man dropped his head and scratched at the dirt between his boots. He sighed. "Ten. Maybe fifteen. But don't get the idea all of them's gonna fight. They ain't. I just got that many to promise to come to Chub's. When I got the message from Patience, I knew things was gonna bust. I got what I could. I'm sorry, Coy."

"It's all right. I didn't think my being with you would help. They need a leader. But they won't follow me because I turned my coat in the war."

Quillen's voice was bitter. He spat the end of the cigarette to the ground, poked it into a hole.

A stone rolled behind them and, before either man could move, a voice cut the growing quiet. "Ain't nobody followin' you, Quillen. But lots of folks'll go with Kewpie."

Chub Willets slid down the Fault side, stopped in front of Coy. The surly man's bearded face hid his thoughts.

"Hello, Chub," Coy said quietly.

"What I said—folks will follow Kewpie. And you're it. Your pulin' brother's worse than nothin'. So you're it. Now let's get to it."

"Now wait, Chub," Davey said, rising.

"You stay outta this, Davey," Willets said. "I ain't making trouble. I'm here to help. You call the way and I'll do whatever God'll let me. But we ain't friends, Quillen. We ain't now and we ain't ever gonna be."

"That's fair enough, Chub. Let's go to work." Coy turned to Davey. "Dave, you scout up to the Army post on foot. Stay in the Fault about a hundred yards and you'll meet a shallow draw. That'll take you to within a fifty-foot piece of the orderly room building. The log one. That's the one we want. Chub and I'll be there with the wagon. And be careful. I started a ruckus over there a while back, but it'll help."

"What's this Army camp business?" Willets asked.

Coy turned to Davey, who was tightening his gun rig, checking his clothing. "Davey, how many more could we get if we had good arms? Henry repeating rifles—all we need?"

The young man grabbed at Quillen's arm. His lean face, stark in the moonlight, was filled with a clean excitement for the first time since Coy had known him. "Henrys? You're not foolin', Coy?" He shook the arm. "How many?"

Coy laughed. "Enough," he said. "Turn me loose and get a-goin'. We'll recruit us an army yet."

"I'll bring the wagon down," Chub Willets said.

Coy couldn't tell in the pale light, but it seemed to him the man's lips held a reluctant smile.

Bringing the wagon close to the building to transport the stolen rifles to it was a harrowing experience. Coy thought the squealing axles and the jangle of equipment must surely reach the ears of the camp. They got the wagon positioned before activity had leveled off at the post. Quillen, lying on the cooling plain beside Davey Forrestor, watched the orderly room. A light burned in the front part. In the rear, De Puys's office, it was dark and silent.

"De Puys must have gone," Quillen said, low-voiced.

"He did," Forrestor answered. "I saw him ride off with his belly bouncin' just after I got here. They was runnin' around over there like a bunch of kids at a picnic. What did you do, Coy?"

Quillen grunted, didn't answer, studying the subsiding activity of the cavalry post. His eyes followed the slow march of the orderly room sentry. The man walked at attention, looking neither to left nor right, up and down in front of the building.

"Got to take care of the yellow-leg," Davey muttered.

"I'll get him," Quillen said. "You just do like we planned. You and Chub come to that window." He pointed to the rectangular blob of light facing them. "That way, only one of us is really exposed to the camp. The tents're in the other direction. I'll hand the guns out the window. You carry them to the wagon."

Quillen took care of the sentry. He didn't want to injure the soldier, so he merely pulled the man behind the building, muffling his shouts, and knocked him out with one sledging blow. Then he trussed him quickly and slid around the corner into the orderly room.

They transferred fifty of the racked Henrys to the wagon without incident. On the floor under the gun racks, Quillen found shot-lockers with Henry ammunition. They took enough for their needs.

They pulled the wagon into the churned-up yard of Chub Willets' Broken-W two hours later. Coy, having lost his horse, rode the wagon with Willets. Neither man had spoken during the long ride.

The Broken-W was a tight, clean ranch with solid-appearing buildings and everywhere evidences of growth. It was in contrast to the man. A low building, long and rambling, of planed lumber, commanded the clearing. A huge stone chimney breathed thin smoke upward. Coy, sweeping his eyes over the house and the outbuildings, noticed small movements at the doors and windows. He nudged Willets, asked a silent question.

"Guns," the man said laconically, drawing the heaving horses to a halt in the dooryard. "They just want to be sure we're friendly. There's a heap of folks in there."

"Chub," Quillen said when the man would have climbed down from the wagon. "I want to thank you for coming tonight."

Willets stopped, looked at him. There was no readable expression on the rough face.

"What I mean is, Chub, you're the type of man Sam Quillen had in mind for this country. I wanted you to know that. That's all."

Willets jumped to the ground, reins in hand. He put a hand on the near wheel, looked up at Quillen. He jerked his head toward the house. "Save your speeches for them."

CHAPTER 16

"I'LL TELL you one thing," Silas Linyard shouted. "Ain't no way in the world I'm gonna bleed behind a son-of-a-bitch wears a coat like that!"

"Now, Si," Davey said.

Several other voices raised at once and the warm, low-ceilinged kitchen of the Willets's house became full of noise. Coy stood, back to a broad roof-pillar, watching the flow of emotion in the room. He wished he could remove the coat. It was hot. The talk went on.

"Si," Coy said, raising his voice above the din. "Silas Linyard. Listen to me!"

His great voice silenced them. It was an uneasy silence. Coy stepped out from the pillar and looked at the upturned faces. The only light came from a roaring fire in the flat-stone hearth. Men sat about on the floor, filled the few chairs; some crowded on the corner bunk Chub undoubtedly had for one of his older boys. There were no women present. Davey stood next to Coy, waiting for his friend to speak.

"I don't know all the different reasons that brought you men here tonight. I do know this—you knew I'd be here. And still you came." Quillen stopped, looked slowly around the room, meeting every eye that challenged him. "We either got a lot to do together, or nothing at all. Whichever, there ain't no time for name-calling and arguing."

"Let's get on with it," George Beech said from the table.

Quillen turned to him. Beech was a farmer from the town-site periphery. Conroy's encroachment threatened him and he had sense enough to know it. Coy knew him slightly.

"All right, Mr. Beech," he said. "I'll put it real simple." He looked around, found all attention centering on him. "Some of you may have the idea we're gonna make war. Well, that's exactly what we're gonna do."

"Hear, hear," Davey cried. A few men echoed him.

"Wait. There's a time for cheers when the deed is done. We must take over Case County and establish citizen control until someone from General Sheridan's headquarters can look into the mess."

"Damn Sheridan!"

"What do we need the Yankee bastards fer?"

"Listen!" Coy pleaded. "Listen, men. We have to do it right. Or all the blood is wasted. Conroy won't just give up this empire he's built. All this wealth and power. He won't give it up without a fight."

"Maddux is the fighter," George Beech said.

Davey nodded. Several others added low-voiced comments.

"Maybe," Coy went on. "But we don't have to worry about him. What we ..."

"Don't have to worry about Maddux?" A small man in a very dirty sheepskin coat stood up. He had a tiny face, seemingly bunched together on the front of his skull. "I'm Sincere Everest, Mr. Quillen. My brother rides for Conroy."

"Sincere has a horse ranch over north, Coy," Davey said.

"As I said," the man continued, "my brother, Tal, he rides for that Conroy snake. Only reason I ain't been scared out. Or burned out. Anyway—Tal's bad. Real bad and always was ... But even he says he can't hold a match to that white-headed dung-worm, Maddux. Wasn't for him, Conroy'd run."

"I'll take care of Maddux," Coy said. It dropped into a lull and stretched into a vibrant hush.

"You'll…" Chub Willets began and trailed off.

"Wait, Coy," Davey Forrestor said. He stepped forward. "You men see what he's doin', don't you? He thinks he has to prove himself. He thinks because of the war he's gotta show us he's on our side."

Coy shouldered him aside. He raised his hands to stop the sudden babble.

"That's not it at all. We're gonna fight, all of us. Somebody has to get Maddux and I think I can handle him. Half of you wouldn't be here if you thought you'd have to face Harley Maddux." He paused, looked around. "So I'll take him—and I'll kill him."

Silas Linyard stood. "Ain't none of us gunslicks, if that's what yer sayin'. But if we can't handle Maddux, how the hell can you— with one arm?"

"Because I have to," Coy said. "Same as you all have to fight. Linyard, I'm tired of your yapping. If you're not with us, get out. The rest of you men listen…"

"Are you sure the Army won't horn in?" Silas Linyard asked when Coy had outlined his simple plan.

Coy scowled at him. He gestured for silence. "No," he said. "I'm not. They shouldn't. De Puys is Conroy's partner. Certainly he'll fight. But he can't order soldiers into a private fight. And that's what it amounts to."

"You sure you talked to that sergeant?"

"You saw the guns, didn't you?"

Sincere Everest moved out of the crowd. The twenty-odd men filled the room pretty well. He stopped in front of Quillen, smiled diffidently.

"We just ain't fighting types, Mr. Quillen. But there comes a time—well, to us you're Kewpie. And Kewpie has always been the big spread. A dollar for a job o' work when the kids needed grub. A place to fill a belly and rub a horse on a ride." He looked around at the quieted group. "You fellows know what I mean. We wouldn't have had guts enough to break out from under Conroy. Now we got the chance. I'm ready."

"What happens when we take the town, Coy?" A kid, sixteen or seventeen with bright, scrubbed features, spoke excitedly from a seat on the floor. "Do we burn up the rest?"

"What's your name, son?"

"Me? Billy Beech," the boy said, uncomfortable in the focus of attention.

"Well, Billy, if I catch you—or anyone—burning anything at all, we'll fight." Coy smiled a little to take the sting from his words. "It's our town. We want it in one piece."

Davey whooped. "Well, let's go get it!"

The men started for the door. A woman's voice shrilled outside and a rifle shot sounded near at hand. Chub held up his hand. "That's my woman," he said. "Someone's out there!" He ran to the front door and swung it wide. He shouted, but Quillen couldn't hear what was said. Coy fought through the crush, made the door.

"It's a woman," Chub said, sticking his head inside. "Rode a dead-bushed horse here from Circle, she says."

It was Lydia. She moved toward Quillen, seeing no one else. She wore a mackinaw and a man's hat; her riding dress was slashed and cut by brush. Her face was white and strained.

"Coy," she said. "Coy."

He pulled her into the warmth and light. The men were curiously quiet. Coy sensed uneasiness and looked around. Eyes slid away. Throats were cleared. Davey stood beside him, jaw outthrust, his slim body taut.

"By God, they make a pair," someone said, sarcasm dripping.

It was Linyard. Someone else shushed him.

"I had to come," Lydia whispered against him. "I had to."

Coy said, "Wait, Lyd." He walked to Linyard. The man cowered at his approach. But his face held the contempt his body hadn't the strength to back. Coy felt a sweeping flash of frustration. He looked around, seeing the same expression all around him.

It wasn't only Linyard. Quillen turned from the man without a word. These people, these simple close-to-violence, close-to-the-soil people, might someday accept him. Because he had violated only an ideal. Lydia they would never take into their homes or their hearts. Some changes come hard, Quillen knew. Morality being the shifting, elusive thing it was. But a woman's virtue was an absolute condition. That's the way it always had been, the way it always would be.

He walked back to the girl, smiled shortly.

"What is it, Lyd? We've got a job to do and no time for distractions."

"I tried to find you at Circle." She spoke without looking at him, eyes fixed on the floor. She knew what the byplay had been about. "I talked to Patience. She told me what happened, where you were. Conroy wants to make a deal. He'll talk water rights with anyone that'll listen. And he says he has a job for you—running Kewpie."

Coy shook his head.

"He's heard about Forty Miles riding to Sheridan," Lydia said. "De Puys is the one that's scared. Conroy wants to talk to you. Somewhere they heard a military inspector is coming."

"Why'd he go to you, young lady?" George Beech asked.

"That's a silly question, George," another put in.

"Sure is," Silas Linyard offered.

"Wait," Davey Forrestor said. His face was stern. "You fellas think what you please. But be mighty careful what you say."

Lydia stepped into the firelight, shrugging away from Quillen.

"You all know me," she said clearly. "I know that by the way you look at me. You think I'm a bad woman. Well, I can't help what you think. And I can't help what I think of you. You're smug, all of you. None of you are the man you should be or you wouldn't lick boots and cringe from outlaws." She stopped, gathered breath. "Lie around and let murders go unpunished and renegades steal your land. You look down on me. Well, go ahead and sneer. Do anything that makes your meager little hearts happy. But help Coy Quillen."

The fire snap was loud in the room. Lydia looked from face to face; no eyes met hers. Quillen moved up beside her. His face was dead, the lips drawn tight.

Nobody said anything.

The sun was dropping low behind a hill when the cavalcade left the Broken-W. Quillen rode at the head of the small column. He glanced back. About as far from a fighting force as you could get, he guessed. Old men and wet-eared boys, handling the Henrys as if they might just bite. He shook his head, turned back to the trail. Lydia rode beside him, muffled in the collar of the mackinaw. They hadn't spoken since the scene in the Willets's kitchen.

He jabbed a heel and his mount lifted into a bumping trot. Chub, morose and uncommunicative, urged his horse up alongside. Davey pounded up on the other.

Quillen twisted in the saddle, shouted to his straggling command. "All right, tighten it up! We'll be in town just after dark."

Davey grinned at him, shook his shoulders. Coy pulled his mount closer to the lean puncher.

"Scared?"

Davey considered it. Then he nodded.

"We'll make it," Coy said grimly. "Maddux is the big one. Conroy won't fight at all."

They rode for a while without speaking. Chub fell back to bring the stragglers into a tighter group. No use making a bigger dust cloud than was absolutely necessary. Sincere Everest, pinched face drawn with fatigue, galloped up to the head of the column.

"Mr. Quillen!"

Coy reined in. Davey raised a hand, then the men halted.
Everest kneed his mount close to Quillen.

"Some of the men want a palaver, Mr. Quillen," the little man
said apologetically. "I told 'em to keep quiet and follow you, but—
well, some of them think we oughta talk to Conroy. In case he's
got a deal we might take. About the water."

Coy said nothing. Several riders edged closer. Everest rubbed
a reddened hand on his neck, turned his eyes away from Quillen.

"We know he won't give back Kewpie. But maybe he'll make
the rest of us a deal for water. Let us cart it from Kewpie Lake,
maybe." He looked up. "I'm just telling you what they think. They
say if Conroy wants to deal, he's scared. And if he's scared, why
do we have to push a fight?"

"What do you say, Sincere?"

"I'm with you, Mr. Quillen. All the way."

"All right. We'll talk." He turned, raised in the stirrups.
"We'll light and rest," he shouted. "Over there."

He pointed to the west where a pitiful group of loblolly pine
and scrub oak pushed upward.

"All right," he said, when they'd all reached the trees. "You
want talk. You'll get it."

He pivoted, pulled his rifle from the saddle boot. He gestured
with it.

"You want to know why we have to fight. I'll tell you." He
reached into a coat pocket, came out with a handful of rags and
strips of rawhide. "You think Conroy might be scared enough to
deal. You're wrong. He needs a little time. Nothing more. He can
crush us if we let him fight like he wants to."

He looked around; each face came under his gaze and each
held its own expression.

"It's as simple as that." While he talked, Coy began wrapping
the stiffened fingers of his right hand with a layer of linen. The
men watched, interested suddenly. "One thing more. We have a

petition in Santa Fe right now. You know about that. Forty Miles took it to Sheridan. He'll send an inspecting officer."

"What makes you think he will?" Beech asked.

Coy pulled the last wrap around his curved little finger. He laid the rifle, the bright, new Henry, carefully in the separately wrapped fingers where the crippled members curved; the thumb remained free. He looked up at Beech.

"Can't afford not to," he said. "His job is to administer the fifth district. His military governor here is a proxy for him."

"De Puys?"

"De Puys. Lydia, help me with this." Coy held out his hand with the rifle balanced on the curved fingers.

"What do you want me to do, Coy?" Lydia asked. She took the hand, looked at Quillen.

He told her how to tie the rifle to the weak hand while the company watched. Lydia threaded pieces of linen in and around each stiff finger; ran strips around the rifle barrel, tied each off tightly around the thick wrist.

"If you don't understand now," Quillen said wearily, "you never will. As the situation stands, De Puys can control any investigation. He's still an officer in good standing. The investigator will go to him first. If we take over, everything will come out. The agreement with Judge Holman, De Puys's crookedness, the greed of our own merchants—all of it. Because we'll make De Puys commit himself now."

He took a piece of rawhide, slit at one end, slipped it over the thumb of his right hand. It was the only digit unwrapped. Coy moved it up and down. It moved, but there was no strength in the grip of it. "And that will be enough," he said. He pulled the rawhide down, forcing the thumb to make a fist around the wrapped fingers and the gun; took turns around the whole thing, over the wrist, loops around the barrel of the Henry. Then he held it out to Lydia to tie off. When it was done, he looked up. His left hand reached down and racked the rifle, sliding a cartridge into the chamber.

"I'm going in," he said, and turned to his grazing mount. He swung aboard, holding the rifle high. Without looking back he started off toward town.

Davey raced for his horse. Chub Willets stood scowling at the crowd. He spat a word. A single word. Then ran for his mount.

"By God," George Beech said. "By the great green God! If he can go after Maddux with that..."

Coy didn't hear the rest. He put his horse to a trot. After a moment, he looked back. Every man was mounted and riding. Right behind. And in every man's hand was a gun, bright and new.

Smoky dusk covered their advance on the unsuspecting town. A mile from Two Trees Quillen called a halt and sent Lydia on ahead with Billy Beech. The boy was to drop the girl at Morly's, then look around the town, reporting back with any information he might pick up.

Coy shrugged in his uniform coat. He lifted his right hand, heavy with rifle, and massaged the fingers through the bindings. The men were silent. They'd done all the talking. Now they'd fight. As best they could.

Coy closed his eyes. The night pushed back and lights pinwheeled on his closed lenses; his nostrils opened and the sweet prairie smell came to him. The smells were good. The breeze was refreshing on his hot body. He felt tight and well-joined and capable. It had been this way in battle. Or just before. The knowledge that shortly you might die affects a man strangely.

"You ready, Quillen?" Chub asked, moving up silently. "Kid's coming back."

Ready? Yes, he was ready. He signaled.

CHAPTER 17

THEY RODE in quietly. Slouched in their saddles, rifles gripped tightly in sweating hands. Two Trees was alive in the covering night. Noise and light poured from the doors of the Drover's Rest; the Mercantile across the way spilled yellow rays through its busy doors to the rutted street. Up and down the sidewalk planks townspeople walked. Unaware. No alarm came.

Coy looked at his strange complement for the last time. He hoped they remembered their orders. They had met Billy Beech a half mile north of town and Coy hadn't halted the column; the Beech kid had related his news riding alongside.

The town was curiously empty of Conroy men, the boy had reported. He had entered the Drover's Rest, had a drink. Harley Maddux was there with another rough-looking character the boy hadn't recognized. Billy had asked for Conroy and been told the dapper little crook was at the ranch with most of his men.

Quillen immediately reset his plans. If they could arrange a coup in the town, they would be in the position they needed. Then when the inspector arrived, there would certainly be a situation to look into. And a stink even De Puys couldn't cover.

But first there was Harley Maddux.

Half of the men under Chub Willets and George Beech continued past the Drover's Rest. The rest, except for Davey and Quillen, began scattering at the square. They would dismount and cover both sides of the street from the square to the saloon. Billy Beech rode just out of town on the road to Kewpie. If Conroy came down with his men, the warning would reach Quillen in time to arrange a welcome.

They were as ready as they ever would be. Coy was satisfied.

"Let's go, Davey," he said.

The pair pushed their animals to a trot. Down the rutted Main Street and into the alley alongside the Drover's Rest. Coy swung to the ground, slapped the horse and stepped quickly around to the high porch of the saloon. He vaulted up, holding the bound rifle high. Davey was right behind, his Colt drawn and ready. The two men stood at the door for an instant, gathering thought and banishing nerves.

"One on each side," Davey muttered. He moved his head, stretching his neck nervously. His jaw muscles were rigid lines.

Coy nodded. "I go left. You go right. Got it?"

"Yeah. Balcony guard?"

"He's yours. Let's go."

They stepped into the noise and confusion of the Drover's Rest in full evening swing. The shotgun guard on Coy's side turned at their entrance. He recognized Quillen, started to swing up the Greener and the butt of Quillen's rifle smashed his open mouth. He crumpled without a sound.

Coy wheeled, eyes searching for Maddux. The gunman stood at the bar, talking to a stocky puncher.

In that instant several actions intermingled. A woman screamed, high and piercing. Behind Coy, a shot sounded somewhere in the room. Quillen had to trust that Davey fired it, keep his eyes on the dangerous pair at the bar. Maddux began to turn, right hand dropping toward his holstered Colt.

"Freeze, Maddux," Quillen shouted.

The bartender reached instead. Quillen snapped a shot, racked the Henry as the man fell, shoulder-shot. All movement stopped within Coy's vision. Maddux stood half-crouched, just beginning his turn. His pale eyes found Quillen in the mirror. He didn't move.

The gun guard on the balcony came alive. He ran along the platform, slamming shots downward without aim. Quillen saw him from the corner of his eye. There was nothing he could do. The guard's gun leveled toward Quillen as he raced across the long balcony. Davey Forrestor fired.

The shot snapped spitefully. The guard ran right on—through the flimsy railing and out into the air. His legs kept moving though there was nothing under him. He dropped, pinwheeling, and crashed into the faro layout, tumbling the lookout chair, smashing the table.

Hell came unglued.

Coy, his body bent slightly at the knees, his rifle boring inexorably on Harley Maddux, shouted for order. Shots and screams were his answer. And then suddenly, inexplicably, the room quieted.

"Quillen!" Maddux said in the hush. "Give me an even break...."

The stocky man next to the foreman stirred. Behind Quillen, Davey spoke reassuringly, reporting the door covered, the room secured. Coy watched both men at the bar.

"Your piggin' string's too short, Harley," he said softly. "This is one you won't tie off."

"Wait," the man said. He licked his lips, the pale eyes searching for an out. "Give a guy a chance, Quillen. You're holdin' on me."

The stocky man made his move. Quillen had been expecting it. The man drew under cover of his turned position and whirled, thumbing the hammer. He died spinning. Coy snapped the shot, saw it strike and whipped the Henry's muzzle back to Maddux, racking home a new load in the same motion. He tensed, waiting for the foreman's move.

None came.

"Conroy's at the ranch," Maddux said, eyeing Quillen in the mirror. "He's leading a party after you. You can trap him if you know where to go. I'll tell you."

"Turn around, Maddux!"

The man turned. His face was gray. His hat toppled off the back of his head and the colorless hair gleamed in the reflected light of the candle-wheels.

"Quillen, wait," he said. His hands pushed outward. "Don't send me out like this. Let me fight."

"You've got a gun."

"I can't draw before you pull that trigger! Let me … give me a …"

Quillen's finger tightened.

"The chance you gave Anse Prinell?"

Maddux knew he was dead then. The knowledge gleamed in his eyes. The world had narrowed to these twenty feet.

"Put your hands down," Quillen ordered. The puzzled man obeyed. "Get ready to draw!"

Maddux straightened. He had courage of a sort. His eyes stuck, fascinated, to the rock-steady barrel of the Henry. His thin lips quirked.

"It's murder, drawin' against a cocked rifle. But if it's all the chance I got …"

Quillen dropped the muzzle of the Henry, his eyes never leaving the gunman. He squeezed off a shot into the floor at his own feet. The rifle pointed floorward, unloaded.

"Draw!" Quillen spat.

Maddux flashed into movement, hand dipping. Coy moved with practiced deliberation; his left hand found the lever, racked the rifle as the bore moved up to center the foreman's breast-bone. The fluid action got the rifle in line and loaded at the same instant that Maddux's Colt came clear of the leather. Both men fired. Smoke belched and eddied.

Maddux buckled, slammed against the bar by the force of the Henry's ball. Quillen was untouched. He twisted, shouted to Davey to hold the place, disarm everybody. Then he walked unsteadily to the door, needing air.

Now they had a town to defend.

Outside, the confusion had settled into sporadic shots and running heels on boardwalks. Coy stumbled to the porch, breathed deeply. A man shouted from the Mercantile. His words were lost, but Quillen chopped a hand in acknowledgment. Someone had started a fire with crates and barrels in the park. Flames leaped before the two old trees, threw dancing shadows on the buildings behind. "All right, Quillen," Coy muttered. "Let's tighten and tail off."

He raised a shout and Davey trotted to him. They signaled. Sincere Everest, his squeezed face alive with enthusiasm ran lightly from Canadian House. Chub drifted up and stood, square-jawed, saying nothing.

"Nothing to it," Everest said.

"Now we've got to hold it," Coy said. "Chub, get as many men as you can and throw a barricade across the street... there." His rifle pointed to the downstreet end of the Drover's long porch.

Davey pulled on him. "They won't come that way, Coy. They'll come through the square. From Kewpie."

Quillen silenced him with a look. A burst of firing came from down the street. Three horsemen raced up, slid their mounts to a stop before the group.

"Found Bland," one of them said. "Him and that blond deputy. They're out of it."

Coy nodded. "Chub, use wagons for that barricade."

Willets jerked his head, started off.

"Wait. Get what bales and stuff can be used from Bradford's. Build it high enough to ..."

"Tom Bradford's raisin' hell already, Mr. Quillen," a ragged man offered.

"Don't worry about him. Take what you need. Leave a two-or three-foot space next to the porch right here. Stick a barrel in it, or something. Got it?"

"I got it," the bearded man said and left.

"Sincere." The little man stepped to the front of the growing crowd in the street. "You get all the horses. All of them. Get 'em into the alley by the Drover's Rest. Behind the barricade."

Everest left at a dead run. Coy turned to Forrestor.

"Everything all right inside?"

"Tight, Coy," Davey said.

"Fine," Quillen said, turning. "George! George Beech ... over here!"

Coy fumbled fresh loads into the Henry while his eyes searched everywhere, trying to probe each shadow, guess each possible contingency, bulwark every weak spot in his little domain. They would come around the square.

"Right here, Coy," George Beech said, climbing the wooden steps. The old man's whitening beard glistened with moisture. His gait was firm, untired.

"George, get some men and drag crates and burning stuff to the fire. Start another at this side of the park. Light from both sides. Put two good men on each pile. Understand?"

"By the fire. All right."

"Don't build 'em up high until the last possible second. Billy will let us know when they're close. Tell the men to wait as long as they can. Then pile everything on the blaze and fall back to either side of the street. Along the walks toward the barricade."

"Right, Captain!"

Coy accepted the promotion with a quick grin. He prodded the old man with his rifle muzzle.

"Get on," he growled.

"Most of them are here, Coy." Forrestor nodded at the street where thirty or more ragged men, clutching rifles and other arms, milled quietly. "Just tell them what to do."

"All right, men," Quillen said, stepping forward. "This is the spot we've got to hold. And we will. All of you get something white—anything, piece of shirt, rag—so we'll be identifiable in the dark."

A man called, "They's some ladies' stuff in the store, Quillen."

The men whooped.

"That's it," Coy shouted, grinning in the firelight. He turned to Davey, the grin sliding off. "Get the lights out inside there. Take six men. Good ones—best you know. Get up on the roof here ... and over there."

"This's two stories."

"The roof, Davey." Coy stepped to the edge of the porch, looked around for a long moment. "Davey. Put two men on Bradford's roof. You take the other four up on the Drover's roof."

"Coy. That's not enough men to do any good."

Quillen jumped to the street, strode rapidly. Davey ran after him. Chub Willets had his barricade well underway. A tumbled hay wagon formed the nucleus, almost choked the space between the high porches. A dozen men scurried busily from Bradford's store to the growing bulwark, carrying barrels and bales and whatever else came to hand. All became part of the wall. One space, about three feet across, remained clear where the barricade met the heavy plank porch of the Drover's Rest.

Coy stood and surveyed the job. His right hand still held the rifle and the binding had begun to chafe. He rubbed it without thinking. Chub leaped from the hay wagon, landed beside Quillen as Forrestor hurried up. The stocky rancher cocked an eye at his project, then turned to Coy.

"Real good, Chub," Quillen said. "You must have been a sapper."

"Confederate sapper," the man said, steady gaze on Quillen.

Coy nodded. They'd never forget. And it was no use entertaining any other idea.

"Chub," Coy said, "get white armbands on your men. Put 'em behind the mess. Check cartridges and roll a barrel of water back there. Tell them to pick their targets ... and *don't get rattled!*"

"What's to keep Conroy from makin' a big circle? Comin' up Main Street from the plains side and trappin' us behind that pile o' junk?"

"Me," Quillen said and walked away.

Davey Forrestor trotted after him. "Captain Quillen," he said. "If it wouldn't be too much trouble…"

Coy stopped. He turned. Davey's face held a tight smile, warped by fatigue.

"Coy, I want to fight. Put somebody else on that roof."

"It's important, Davey, and I want you up there."

Forrestor looked at him for a long moment, eyes searching. Then he sighed. "O.K. If you say so. What do I do?"

"Stay at the back. Don't fire off the front at all. They'll…"

"That's where they'll come—the front."

Quillen shook his head. "Yes. The first time. It'll cost them. They won't try it twice. Someone will remember the alley running alongside the Drover's Rest. It opens behind the barricade. They'll try to get through it." He smiled, punched Davey with the rifle. "You stop 'em from up there."

Sincere Everest ducked through the hole in the homemade wall and joined them. His little bowed legs scissored. He waved a greeting, almost a salute.

"Horses where you wanted 'em, Mr. Quillen."

"Good, Sincere." Coy rubbed his forehead. The time was running out. "Now, Sincere," Quillen said. "You ride pretty well, Davey tells me. That right?"

"Well, I'm a fair hand, Mr. Quillen. I kin stick one."

"Get eight more good horsemen. Make sure they have both rifles and pistols. Mount 'em and hold 'em in that alley. Have a horse for me. Don't get in the fight until I tell you where to go."

"All right, Mr. Quillen. Pick anyone I want?"

"Yes…" Quillen noticed that everywhere his eyes fell there were men with white patches on their sleeves. By the fire, at the barricade, running up and down the steps of the Rest. "Where'd we get all these people?"

Sincere Everest grinned, exposing brown teeth. "Some o' the towners don't like Conroy no better'n we do. And some we volunteered." He turned, flung words over a shoulder. "I'll have them cavalries, Mr. Quillen."

Coy checked his installation with his eyes. What he could have done with one little Napoleon! And cannister. But this was just as much a war. He started toward the Mercantile and the shout came, rolling out from the watcher at First Street.

A faraway rumble. The drumming of hoofs drifted to the suddenly silent town. Coy knew the time had come—well, they were ready; his quick eyes took in the purposeful preparations for battle. He broke into a run, swinging the rifle over his head in signal.

"Hold that fire!" he shouted. "Hold it 'til …"

And then there was no breath for shouting. Lydia ran out of First Street, hair streaming, riding skirt billowing out behind. She looked around wildly, silhouetted by firelight.

"Here!" Quillen called. "Down here!" And started for her.

The girl ran into his arms. He held her for a moment. Lydia pushed herself away. Her eyes were strangely shadowed.

"Why'd you come out here?" he asked, doubly harsh because of his fear for her. "I told you to stay at the Morlys'."

"Yes, Coy, but I couldn't. Not when Mother let slip about Bud." She looked down, smoothed her skirt with fidgety movements. "You had to know."

"Bud?" Coy shook her with his good hand. "Know what? Tell me. Conroy's almost here. What about Bud?"

"He was in the Drover's when you shot Maddux. He went out the back door—to Morlys'. He took a horse, said something about he had to find Conroy …"

Coy raised his head. The rumbling was steady now, grew louder as they stood in the fire-splashed street. Quillen's face felt hot; the skin too small to cover it. The drumming sound swelled.

"Did you hear me, Coy," the girl said, raising her voice. "Bud went looking for Conroy!"

"He found him," Coy said quietly.

CHAPTER 18

I T WAS THUNDER, growing in the night. Coy broke away from Lydia, trotted to the center of the street. His searching gaze took in the preparations. They hadn't had much time, but everything was in order. George Beech ran toward him down the street. He pulled up alongside Quillen, snorting from the exertion and excitement.

"Ready," he wheezed. "They'll pile that stuff just before Conroy hits the square. They can see a piece up First Street."

"Good. Get four men—any four men—and get in the Mercantile. Defend from there. Tell your men to pick targets, fire slowly."

Chub had his men in place. Rifles poked over, under and between portions of the jerry-built wall. Chub himself sat high on a wheel of the capsized hay wagon, checking his complement with experienced eyes. He nodded to Coy, spat tobacco into the street.

"We'll do all right," he grunted.

Quillen listened. The rumble had changed to a rata-plan out of which individual beats could be heard. They were close. "Sounds like a thousand," he said. His throat was suddenly dry and the rifle bound to his hand grew heavier.

Chub cocked his head. "Does," he agreed. He swung his sullen eyes over the wall, noted muzzles poking from the Drover's Rest, the Mercantile; he raised up, found the small mounted group where they waited in the beginning shadow of the alley's mouth. "Won't be many ride away," he said and scrambled behind the wagon.

"Coy!" The cry was shrill. Quillen realized he had left Lydia standing when the alarm came. He gestured with the Henry.

"Get out of here!" He ran toward her. "Go on—get back to Morlys'!"

"They don't want me," she cried. "They're uncomfortable when I'm there. If it wasn't for Mother, I wouldn't get in the door. Coy, I belong with you. Give me a gun. You may as well, I'm not leaving you."

He protested, then realized the girl could not go back to the doctor's house in any case. It was on First Street to the west—and that was the direction from which Conroy was coming. He grasped her arm roughly.

They ran to the side of the barricade where the hole had been left, ducked through. Behind, it was darker; the wall cut off all but the highest of the flame's reflections. He pulled her to the walk, up and into the doorway of a building beyond the alley. It was a restaurant, dark and shuttered now. He pounded on the door. A frightened woman opened it a crack and Coy shoved Lydia inside.

"Coy! Be careful," the girl said before the closing door separated them.

A crackle of gunfire broke out at the square. An instant later, a torrent of horsemen, firing as they came, poured around the corner into Main Street. They raced for the barricade.

The flames reached higher into the night sky and the defender's guns spoke in rasping coughs. The firelight made it target practice. The Henrys spat and horsemen fell.

Coy ran at the wall, leaped. He stood high on the barricade, exposed to the return fire, yelling at the top of his lungs, loading and firing.

The attack broke. Conroy had come on without plan, thinking to overrun the few foolish farmers and ranchers. Four bodies lay in the fire-lit street, mute testimony to the determination of the defenders. Several more had ridden off, clinging to saddle horns.

A cheer rose from Quillen's men. Chub Willets turned to Coy and made a face, almost smiled. He spat instead.

"We've got a minute," Coy shouted. "Take a breath. They won't get organized for a minute."

He jumped to the street. The horsemen at the alley had their hands full, controlling noise-maddened animals.

The firing settled into sporadic outbursts and intermittent shots. Mostly from the defenders in the Drover's Rest. They had the best angle. Conroy's men had attempted to put out the fires, but they had grown too hot to get close to. But they wouldn't burn forever. Somebody had been bright enough to pull wagons up in the square and alongside the park for cover. Now Conroy's men had gotten behind these impromptu forts and resumed the fight.

Coy ducked as a ball whizzed angrily near him, ticking his hat. He grinned. His eyes searched the attackers. He could recognize none at this distance. Then, as he watched, a huge figure raced from one side of the square clutching a flaming brand. Moriarty! The big man ducked behind a porch post as a hail of lead reached for him.

On the barricade, Chub Willets thrust his body upward, rifle poised. His square jaw worked, crushing his cud. Moriarty jumped up, started forward, swinging his torch. Chub raised higher, sighted carefully and waited, exposed to the increased fire from the square.

"Chub!" Quillen shouted. "Down, you fool!"

A bullet struck the stocky man. He slumped, straightened. Coy froze, watching the spectacle. Moriarty intended to fire the barricade. Straight down the street he ran, ignoring screaming lead.

He had no chance. A hundred bullets must have struck him. Each blow turned him, stopped him; he staggered on. Then Chub Willets poured an entire magazine into the brutal face at killing range.

Moriarty fell with the torch a scant yard from his goal.

The minutes went by. Davey's group on the roof fought off an attempt to circle the Drover's Rest by way of the alley. Both sides sniped spitefully. Little damage was done.

"This could go on and on," Coy muttered. He called for Sincere Everest. "Tell the men to check their rigs. We're going out and end this thing." He slipped to the ground.

Chub Willets, bleeding badly from a wound in his side, met him as he ran along the rear of the barricade. The rancher's homespun shirt was soaked with blood, his beard singed on one side from rifle back-flash. He showed tobacco-stained teeth to Quillen. "Stopped 'em," he said.

"Never mind the speech," Coy said. They both laughed.

From the barricade, men called down to Quillen; good-natured curses and fighting talk. Men do not wear well in siege if they have not been trained to absolute obedience. Quillen knew this. Now they were fine. But it wouldn't last. Every moment that passed strengthened Conroy's chances.

"Chub," he said, "I'm taking Sincere and the horsemen out."

"We'll cover you. That's why you left that there section loose, ain't it? So's you could get out that way?"

"Originally, yes." Quillen ducked as a fresh outburst from the square poured overhead. "We're going out the alley instead. About two hundred yards up First Street is Hanson's livery. It's got a drive all the way through to this alley. We go through there, down First, and on them from the side. Got it?"

"Well, yeah. But what do we do?"

Quillen turned, started off, still talking. Chub trotted after him. "Stop your fire when we enter the square. No use shooting one of us. When you see a horse break down from the square right at you, open the loose section."

"Gonna use it to get in, steada out..."

Quillen knelt briefly, rubbed his good hand with dirt. A man moaned in the darkness near by. Coy stood up, caught at his horse. "Get back in there, Chub," he said. Then, to Everest, "After me."

He threaded his horse through the mounted group, speaking all the way, outlining the plan. The men, mostly young cowchousers, were eager for battle. And most had hot grudges to settle with Conroy and his people.

Coy halted his small force at the livery drive where it turned into First Street. It was dark here. No light at all. The houses were dark, burghers fearing that a gleam would invite the trouble they heard all around them.

"Men," Coy said. "One thing. When I say get out there, that means git! Everybody hit for the hole. If I go down, Sincere will give the orders. All right?"

There was a murmured chorus of assent. A few rifles cocked loudly; creaking leather and nervous curses announced preparation. Then Coy tightened his legs on the surging power under him and clucked. The horse jumped out into the rutted road, wheeled at a pressure from Quillen and bounded down the street toward the enemy. After him came his irregular cavalry, yelling like fury.

They went amongst the Conroy men like a strong gust in a pile of leaves. Coy yelled and swung the Henry, wheeling and dancing his animal over shouting men, around piled debris. He couldn't fire. Not with one arm. If he released the reins, the horse would bolt; as it was, it took all of his considerable strength to manage the plunging animal in the confusion.

"It's Quillen!" a voice shouted.

Bullets began plucking at his clothes. He swung between the trees in the square, dodged the smoldering fires and pounded to the other side of First Street, shouting all the way and flailing at running men with the stock of his rifle.

His troop followed, dealing death and spreading panic through the attackers. Coy saw that the number of men opposing them was much smaller than he'd imagined. He fought abstractedly, searching for Matt Conroy. He didn't see him any-where. Then the tide began to turn against them. Men on foot can fire more carefully than mounted men. One of Quillen's men went down, torn from his saddle by a well-aimed shot. Sincere Everest rode up, shouting.

"Mr. Quillen! It's getting warm."

"All right," Coy said, turning his bucking mount. "Let's go back. Anyone seen Conroy?"

But Everest had leaned over his animal, sent it leaping back across the square. "Let's go!" the little man shouted. "Quillen! All Quillen, let's ride!"

And the troop, what was left of it, thundered past the Canadian House, raced at the barricade. Coy rode with the rest. In a moment they were safe inside and Chub's guns poured a hail of cover for them.

Davey met Quillen as he tumbled from the lathered bay. The young man held him as he would have fallen, pushed him upright.

"Coy. Are you hit? You all right?"

Quillen leaned on the shoulder for a moment. The rifle dragged at his arm like a running cow at a lariat. It seemed to him he had never been without the weight of it.

"I'm all…" He broke off, recognizing the man. "What're you doing down here? Get back up there and watch that alley. How many…"

Davey wrenched away, face tightening. He stalked to the bar-ricade, fingering his rifle. Coy ran after him.

"Davey! We need someone up there."

"Someone," Davey threw back. "Not me. My brother was killed. You recollect that? And my pa. I'm the one who needs to be in it. Right in the middle of it." He turned. The fires in the park had died and the only light was the moon, but the young man's expression was easily read—stubborn conviction and hard anger.

Coy searched for an answer. There was none. He followed the slim puncher. Both climbed the pile, found firing places in the mish-mash of piled bags and bales. Chub waved weakly from his position. The firing had tailed off to almost nothing at all.

Davey wiggled into shooting position, body hanging from an overturned cart. A bullet whanged off a steel tire and ricocheted. Coy ducked his head. He pulled up to where he could see through an aperture. His eyes studied the battleground. And it was all of that. Bodies lay in sprawling indignity; pieces of equipment and burned bits of wood were strewn in mortal disarray.

"A real mess," Quillen muttered.

"Why don't we go out there and finish it," Davey said, not looking at Coy. "One more charge and they'd be done. Scattered. The thievin' Yankee scum!"

"Maybe ..."

"Maybe? There ain't more'n ten of 'em left. Oh, I know—you think I just want to get at Conroy. And that's right. But that ain't why I say another charge'll finish the thing. It will, though. Anyone can see that."

Coy peered into the darkening square. The fires were completely burned out and scattered now. It was impossible to distinguish features from this distance.

"I don't like it. I haven't seen Conroy. And where's De Puys? I don't like it at ....."

The firing from the square stopped abruptly. A ragged cheer rang out from the Conroy men. Coy straightened, pushed head and shoulders above the barricade.

There in the square, in the paling light of the high moon, Captain Peter De Puys sit a cavalry horse like a blue Buddha, hand upraised. The pudgy officer's command rang out in the momentary silence, shouting for everyone to cease firing.

Behind him, line on line, visible past the corner of Canadian House, spread a uniformed troop of United States Cavalry. A slim lieutenant rode along the front rank, saber upheld.

Quillen stood. In that instant, he was older than time, and more tired than Atlas with the world's weight bowing him. He raised his arms.

"Hold your fire!" he shouted. "Everybody! Cease firing. Hold it, boys!"

He stopped, climbed high on the bullet-pocked pile. Something was wrong here. De Puys with soldiers. It just couldn't be. He wouldn't dare commit himself to—Quillen bent suddenly, squatting on the wagonside. He leveled his rifle.

"Fire!" he shouted into the shocked silence. "Give 'em hell!"

A saber swished in the square and a golden tassle floated with the movement. The distance was great, but Coy recognized the set of the head, the erect carriage on the slim lieutenant. The gold-tasseled dress sword was the one his brother had carried away after the argument at Angelarry's!

CHAPTER 19

THE VOLLEY did not come with Coy's order. If it had, De Puys would certainly have fallen. As it was, he coolly wheeled his horse and ordered the blue files back behind the angle of Canadian House where the delayed and poorly aimed shots from the defenders did no damage.

Quillen fired until the heat of the barrel seared his crippled hand. Davey pulled him bodily off the wall. He tumbled to the street, cursing and fighting to load the hot weapon.

"But the Army, Coy!" Davey grasped his arm, his face anguished. "You said..."

Coy stopped. "Davey," he said, and for the first time since the fight had started, his voice was hesitant, unsure. "Davey, I don't know. I just don't. I thought I saw Bud out there. In a uniform. If so..."

"You mean maybe they ain't soldiers?"

Quillen began to nod. A burst of booming Henry shots sounded from the Drover's roof. A thin cry drifted down. The two men started for the open end of the wall. A horseman broke down at them.

"Mr. Quillen!" Sincere Everest, clinging to his plunging horse, haunch-slid his animal to a halt before them. "One got through," he panted. "He's..."

Suddenly his words were unnecessary. A shadowy horseman surged through the alley and galloped out into the moonlit street at their very feet. His head was bare and he rode clutching the far side of the saddle. Coy got a glimpse of a white face, blond hair.

It was Bud Quillen. He wore the regimentals of a Federal trooper. His lips were twisted and he shouted, but his words were lost in the din.

Coy stood immobile. Davey, alerted by Everest, snapped a shot at the horse as it passed. But he missed. Bud spun the animal, somehow managed the maneuver while clinging like an Indian. He rolled off into the street, was up immediately, running straight at them.

"Coy!" he shouted, running. "Hold your fire!"

Quillen came alive, turned. But Davey's ready Colt had centered the charging man; he fired, a tongue of flame lancing out from the pistol's mouth. Coy struck the gun aside.

"Don't, you fool!" He ran to his brother. Bud was down in the street, struggling feebly to rise. His neck where the shoulder joined was a mass of blood.

Coy knelt beside him, lifted the curly head.

The younger Quillen smiled up at his brother. His eyes flashed the old, frivolous gleam and for a moment almost forgot where they were, what was happening. Then a spasm twisted the young man's face.

"Don't talk," Coy said, pushing the matted curls off his brother's forehead. He had his arm around the boy and the rifle—still bound to the hand—lay over Bud's lower body.

"Made your arm longer, didn't you?" the younger Quillen said.

Coy found his voice. "That was a damn fool thing," he said. "We've got a fight here. You could have been killed. Why did you do it?"

"I had to tell you." The smile disappeared. "There are no troops out there, Coy. None. Fourteen men, none of them soldiers. That's all. I waited until I had a chance to break away." His hand came up, clutched Quillen's shirt. "I quit Conroy after that night at the Wells. You got to believe that, Coy."

"I do, Bud. You saved my life."

The boy relaxed. Pain flitted across his white face. He licked his lips. "Let me talk," he said. "When you hit the Rest and downed Maddux, I knew the fight was on. It was whether I could help you more by being with you or by keeping an eye on Conroy. I rode out, met him and the whole crew riding in from the ranch. I told him about Maddux. Told him you had fifty men. He sent me with De Puys and twelve others to the Post for uniforms. When we got there, O'Bain tried to stop us and De Puys shot him."

"O'Bain shot?"

"I don't think it was bad. I knocked up the gun. It just creased him."

"Where's Conroy? We haven't seen him at all."

"He's there," Bud said. His voice was weakening. "All the time, he's been there. From the first."

Coy shifted, got his arm under the boy. He lifted, grunting with the effort. Davey and Sincere, backs to the brothers, stood rifle guard behind them. A shot sounded now and then from the square.

"Wait!" Bud cried. "Let me finish...."

"I got to get you some help," Coy said, walking off with him. "You shut up."

"Coy. Coy, listen. You got to go out there. Now...before they think up somethin'. There can't be more than twenty all together. You..."

They reached the door of the restaurant where Quillen had deposited Lydia. He turned to Davey following. "Take him," he ordered. "Get him inside. Lydia will take care of him."

Davey took the limp weight from Quillen's arms, nodded. Sincere Everest pounded on the door. Coy leaped from the porch, ran to the barricade.

The firing had all but stopped. He found Chub.

"What's happening?"

"Everybody's tired of it, Quillen. I reckon that's it. I am. God damn, I'm tired!"

A bullet whacked into the horse trough. Both men ducked.

"Someone ain't," Quillen said, pulling his stiff face into a grin.

"Yeh, they are," Chub said, turning away. "And we are. Let's do somethin', Quillen. Anything."

"Mr. Quillen." A man at Quillen's left raised his head. "Them's soldiers out there. We ain't got no chance at all."

"They're not soldiers, boys," Quillen answered. He raised his voice so men all along the line could hear. "They're not soldiers. De Puys dressed some of Conroy's gunnies in Army blue. That's all. Hold tight now and we'll all be home for breakfast."

A murmur ran the length of the wall, turned into a weak cheer. It was a vote of confidence.

"You got us into it," an oldster called—a farmer from the look of him said. "Get us out, boy. Get us out."

Coy lifted himself, peered out over the top. The scene was a strange one. No living person showed in the moonlit park and square. Occasional flashes of muzzle fire relieved the gloom. As he watched, a group of blue-garbed horsemen dashed out from behind the Canadian House, thundered across the park and into First Street east. They drew no fire.

De Puys was busy at something. Coy started back. He heard the bugle then, rising in the clear night air, chattering its brass insistence. All activity stopped. They listened. The bugle sang and gradually they heard the sound of many horses traveling rapidly.

A man swore, kept it up with weary repetition. Coy stood on the top of the wall. No one fired at him.

"By God," Chub said. "*That's* soldiers!"

"What now, bright boy?" a voice called.

Quillen turned. He waved his arms to his men. He was smiling broadly, feeling relief surge through him. They'd won! He began shouting it, over and over.

To De Puys, it must have been a nightmare. To stand in the wreckage of a military career to which he'd dedicated his life, directing renegades in a pygmy battle for profit and hear the voice of personal doom, racing over the countryside.

De Puys didn't wait for the Army. He knew what would be his lot at the hands of the uniform he had disgraced. With the first bugle sound he wheeled his mount, rode to the front of the square.

"Men!" he shouted, fighting his plunging horse. "Men ... listen! Here's an issue now. Who'll charge with me? Iron guts, to me! To me!"

A horseman cantered to him. Another. Horses plunged and wheeled. One was Tal Everest. Coy recognized the gunhand. The fat captain raised his voice in a tremendous shout, sent his animal straight at the barricade.

"A De Puys!" he screamed, swinging his saber in wide, glistening arcs. "A De Puys for glory!"

Four men, charging like an army. Coy forgot to move, to get behind the barricade. He was stunned at the wonder of it. Captain Peter De Puys disdained to fire. He put his straining charger at the wall, saber in hand—right at Coy Quillen.

"A De Puys!" The raging officer lifted his mount at the wall and the animal thrust itself, powerful hindquarters bulging with effort. By then the world had gone mad for Quillen and he yelled with the passion of the moment, waited for the curving steel. His rifle raised, but did not fire.

De Puys, screaming invective mixed with his battle-cry, leaned forward as the horse began his leap, reached for Quillen with the bright length of his blade.

The hay wagon saved Quillen. De Puys's charger pushed a leg through the spokes of a canted wheel and fell to the side. The captain twisted, sliding from the saddle, still trying to get his blade in the wide body of the man on the wall. He thrust viciously.

Coy spun, slashed with the rifle, hitting steel.

The two men came together and whirled on the barricade. The trapped horse lashed out in pain and a hoof caught Quillen high on the shoulder. His head spun. He clung desperately to the thick figure of De Puys. Both men teetered on the wall. Quillen strained and jammed his shoulder into the fat neck. They toppled, fell to the rutted street locked together.

Davey's voice went on for some time before Coy could separate the words, make sense of the murmuring. He lay on the earth and the rifle, still bound to his hand, made a hard ridge in his back. His arm was twisted. There was a dull ache behind his eyes. The wind had turned cool. The feel of it on his face brought him awake.

"Coy. Coy, can you hear me?"

Quillen opened his eyes. Davey Forrestor's face seemed far away above him. Then the haze began to clear.

"Coy, listen—the inspector's here. A brigadier. Forty brought him. We're gonna be all right, Coy. We're gonna be all right."

"De Puys?" He tried to sit up. His head spun. "What happened to De Puys?"

"Easy," Davey said. "Easy now. He's dead."

Forrestor helped him up. Coy struggled to his feet, stood weaving.

"When you toppled off the wall, he broke his neck."

He saw him then. Captain Peter De Puys, twisted and puffed like a fat rag doll, lay at the foot of the wall, one arm bent under the gross body. His neck hung oddly.

Coy looked around. The battle was over. Men straggled from the Mercantile, the Drover's Rest. George Beech was stumbling toward them.

"How long was I out?" Coy asked.

"Just a few minutes," Davey said. "Look there."

The square was alive with dismounted cavalrymen. Conroy's men, those still alive, stood in the park, hands elevated. Coy saw the bulky figure of Eldred O'Bain and a quick gladness filled him. The redhead stood beside a slim officer with a gold sash, directing the soldiers. A white bandage circled the Irishman's head. He glanced down the street, waved to Quillen. His bull voice rang out.

"Knew they couldn't kill you!" he shouted. "Be there in a minute, boy. The general here'll clean things up."

George Beech came up, walking old. His beard had been burned completely off on one side by the flash of his weapon. He shook his head at Quillen, blew out his breath in a sigh. "A mighty thanks, Coy Quillen," he said.

"Not to me, Beech. I don't need your thanks."

"Maybe. That may be," the old man said. "But now I'll be driving my thirsty cows to Kewpie. That is, if you're of a mind to share the water as Sam Quillen did. And Anse Prinell."

Coy stood taller. He looked out over the heads of the men gathering around, all trying to show in their weary faces what the past hours had done for and meant to them. He heard the voices and they meant nothing. Any minute now the door would open. The door to a restaurant in a violent town. He watched.

"How about it, Coy?" It was Chub Willets, very much the worse for wear. "We gonna get the water, or ain't we?"

"It's not me you should see. Anybody know what happened to Conroy?"

"Why, he's right there," George Beech said, pointing to the square. "Gave up like a soldier, Matt did."

"Coy," Davey Forrestor said. "Let me get that rifle off your hand."

Quillen had forgotten the thing. He raised it, turned it over, looked up and down the scarred stock and shining barrel. "Tool," he said. He thrust it out to Davey. "Cut it off."

"How about the water, Quillen?" Chub pushed forward. "I fought today. And I can fight some more, if that's the way it's got to be. My stock needs that water. I aim to see they get it."

Quillen didn't look at him. He was watching the figures stride from the square: O'Bain with Conroy in tow, and the brigadier, tailcoat waving, campaign hat alive with gold.

"Don't worry about it, Johnny Reb," Coy said. "You won't have to depend on any Yankee for your water. Bud Quillen will run Kewpie. You ask him. Or Mrs. Prinell, if she'll talk to you."

Davey had finished removing the rifle. He straightened with it in his hand, looked into the set face of his friend. "Now don't get ranny, Coy. You know you don't mean that. You belong here…this is where you fit. You'll feel different when this is forgot."

But some things are never forgotten. Quillen knew that was the way it was.

He punched the rancher lightly. "You just get on a horse and get out to Circle. There's a girl there a hell of a lot too good for you—but she'll have you. I don't know why. Don't worry about me." Conroy, O'Bain, and the general reached the group, passed just beyond. Quillen raised his voice so that all the men could hear. "All right, now you've got your land, your water—whatever the hell it was you wanted. Now leave me alone. All of you! Go away!"

The men gave way before him. They were grave, faces averted. Quillen stopped by O'Bain, stared long and levelly at Conroy.

The little man, still looking dapper somehow, disheveled and grimy as he was, gave a mock bow. "Your hand, Mr. Quillen," he said smoothly. "Your game. Seems as how I bought the wrong Quillen."

Coy shook his head. "No," he said grimly. "This Quillen was bought, too, Matt. And in worthless coin."

The brigadier pushed forward, offered a hand to Coy. "Meredith Pringle, Sheridan's staff," he said. "This young man brought us your petition. From the look of things, you damn near waited too long."

Forty Miles moved up on Coy's left, grinned all over his tanned face. He bobbed his head at Coy, rubbed a hand over his face.

"Forty," Coy said. He threw an arm over the boy's shoulder. "I said you were the man for the job. You did good."

The boy's face flamed. Pringle stirred.

"Well, Mr. Quillen, the Army has a job to do here. I'd better be about it. These people will be thinking all Union officers are like De Puys." He spat into the street. "De Puys. By God—"

"General …"

"Yes?" The officer's epaulets flashed as he turned. "What is it?"

"About the land. Conroy stole land, took property. Him and his phony judge. What about the land?"

"Don't worry," the slim officer said. "A Federal marshal right now is gathering in the Honorable Eustace Holman. He'll be talked to very carefully." He looked around, raised his voice. "All land will be returned to the rightful owners. It may take some time, but it'll be done. My promise. The United States has no desire to steal from its citizens—or allow anyone else to do it. You'll get your land."

A ragged cheer went up. Then the gathering broke up into excited groups. Coy moved to Conroy. The little man stood quietly, his hands hanging loosely. The smile had changed a trifle, but it was still there.

"I don't know what they'll do to you," Coy said, "but good luck."

"And to you, Quillen." Conroy bowed. "You'll be leaving, I guess?"

Quillen nodded, his eyes going to the shuttered restaurant. "Yes," he said. "I'll be leaving. Leaving Kewpie, leaving Texas. A big country full of tiny people."

"Not all of them now, Quillen," O'Bain rumbled. "Not all of them, lad."

"No. Not all. But I'm leaving."

He turned toward the barricade. The door of the restaurant opened. Lydia stood there in the doorway, smoothing her hair. Her eyes searched the crowd until they found him. Then she smiled, stepped out. Her face was pale and strain pulled at the full lips. She saw no one but Quillen.

He waited.

She walked tall, eyes fixed on the man whose life she'd been born to share; her litheness challenged censure, her chin was raised and a blatant promise shone in her eyes.

"You came out a winner, Quillen," Matt Conroy called softly as Coy started for the girl. "The biggest of all."

Meredith Pringle stared after Quillen as he walked to meet Lydia. They turned away and began walking into the breaking day.

"No, Mr. Conroy," the general said. "These people made the winning. The people of Two Trees. Because there was a man like Coy Quillen in their midst."

Coy walked slowly, conscious of Lydia's touch as they moved toward the square. Neither spoke, content to be together, knowing they would always be together. The trees waved in the morning breeze.

The brass tones of Eldred O'Bain rang out over the town. "All right, now. Let's get this mess out of the street. There's a new day comin'..."

www.ingramcontent.com/pod-product-compliance
Lightning Source LLC
Chambersburg PA
CBHW030344180626
46812CB00007B/2754